BATMAN

←YOU CH

DC COMICS
SUPER HEROES

STONE ARCH BOOKS
a capstone imprint

You Choose Stories: Batman
is published by Stone Arch Books,
A Capstone Imprint
1710 Roe Crest Drive
North Mankato, Minnesota 56003
www.mycapstone.com

STAR35644

Cataloging-in-Publication Data is available
on the Library of Congress website.
ISBN: 978-1-4965-3088-2 (library binding)
ISBN: 978-1-4965-3090-5 (paperback)
ISBN: 978-1-4965-3092-9 (eBook pdf)

Summary: Rā's al Ghūl plans to unleash an undead army
on the world to wipe out humanity. With your help,
Batman will track down the super-villain and put a stop to
The Lazarus Plan!

Printed and bound in Canada.
009631F16

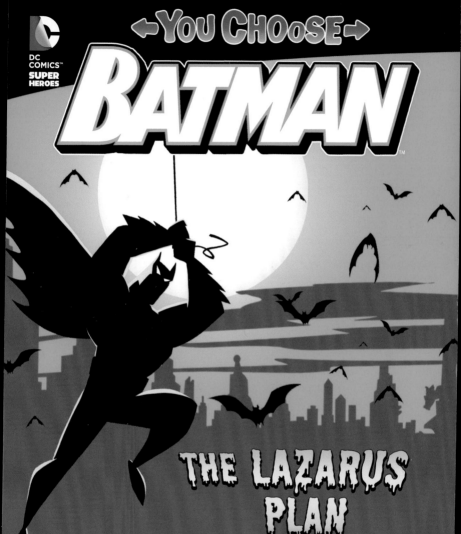

← YOU CHOOSE →

BATMAN™

THE LAZARUS PLAN

Batman created by Bob Kane with Bill Finger

written by
John Sazaklis

illustrated by
Ethen Beavers

DC COMICS™
SUPER HEROES

YOU CHOOSE

BATMAN

The villainous Rā's al Ghūl plans to unleash an undead army on the world to wipe out humanity. Only YOU can help the Dark Knight and his friends track down the super-villain and put a stop to *The Lazarus Plan*!

Follow the directions at the bottom of each page. The choices YOU make will change the outcome of the story. After you finish one path, go back and read the others for more Batman adventures!

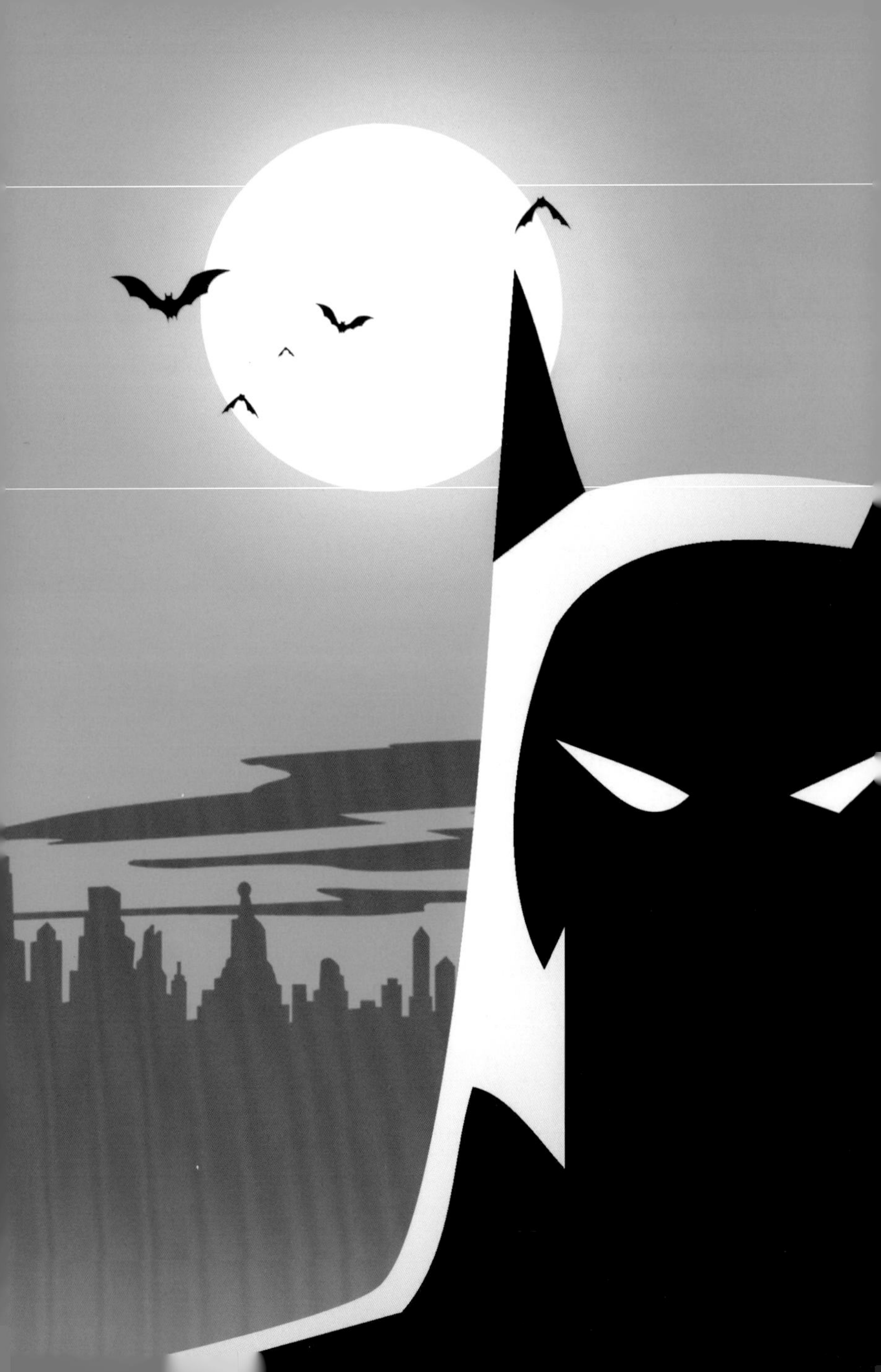

VROOOM!

A sleek black vehicle zooms through the dark city streets. It's the Batmobile, and the driver is none other than Batman—the mysterious guardian of Gotham City.

The car's bright headlights cut through the darkness like twin blades. Batman is investigating a recent blackout, and all clues lead to suspicious activity at the Gotham City Power Plant.

When he arrives, the Dark Knight exits the Batmobile and searches for the culprit. Suddenly, a brilliant flash lights up the night sky. ***KRA-KOOM!*** Bolts of lightning shoot into the air from the roof.

That's a shocking development, Batman thinks to himself.

Turn the page.

He pulls the grapnel gun from his Utility Belt and aims it high. *PAF!* The cable lifts Batman to the roof. His black cape billows behind him like the wings of a bat.

The Dark Knight lands silently on the roof. He comes face to face with the bandit behind the blackout. "I had a hunch you'd be behind this, Maxie Zeus!" Batman says.

Maxie Zeus is a tall, bearded, and muscular man. He wears a toga and holds a metal rod shaped like a lightning bolt. Maxie is a power-hungry madman who believes he's the real Zeus, king of the Greek gods. "Only gods may dwell upon Olympus!" he bellows. "Are you a god?"

"I'm Batman," replies the Caped Crusader.

"So gloomy and dark," says Maxie with a yawn. "You remind me of my brother Hades, ruler of the Underworld."

"Why have you shut down the city's power?" asks Batman.

"To harness it, of course," the madman answers. "Only I shall provide the people of Gotham with electricity … and for a very high price."

"I'm shutting *you* down," Batman says. He reaches into his Utility Belt and pulls out the Bat-cuffs.

Zeus cackles at the sight of them. "Do you think your flimsy shackles can contain my power?" The villain aims the lightning rod as it crackles with energy. "It's time you saw the light, Batman!" he yells.

ZZZARK! Pulsing blasts of electricity shoot out at the hero.

Batman backflips out of the way as the lightning bolts hit the fire escape ladder. ***ZAP! BOOM!***

"Well done. But I'm just getting warmed up!" laughs Zeus.

Turn the page.

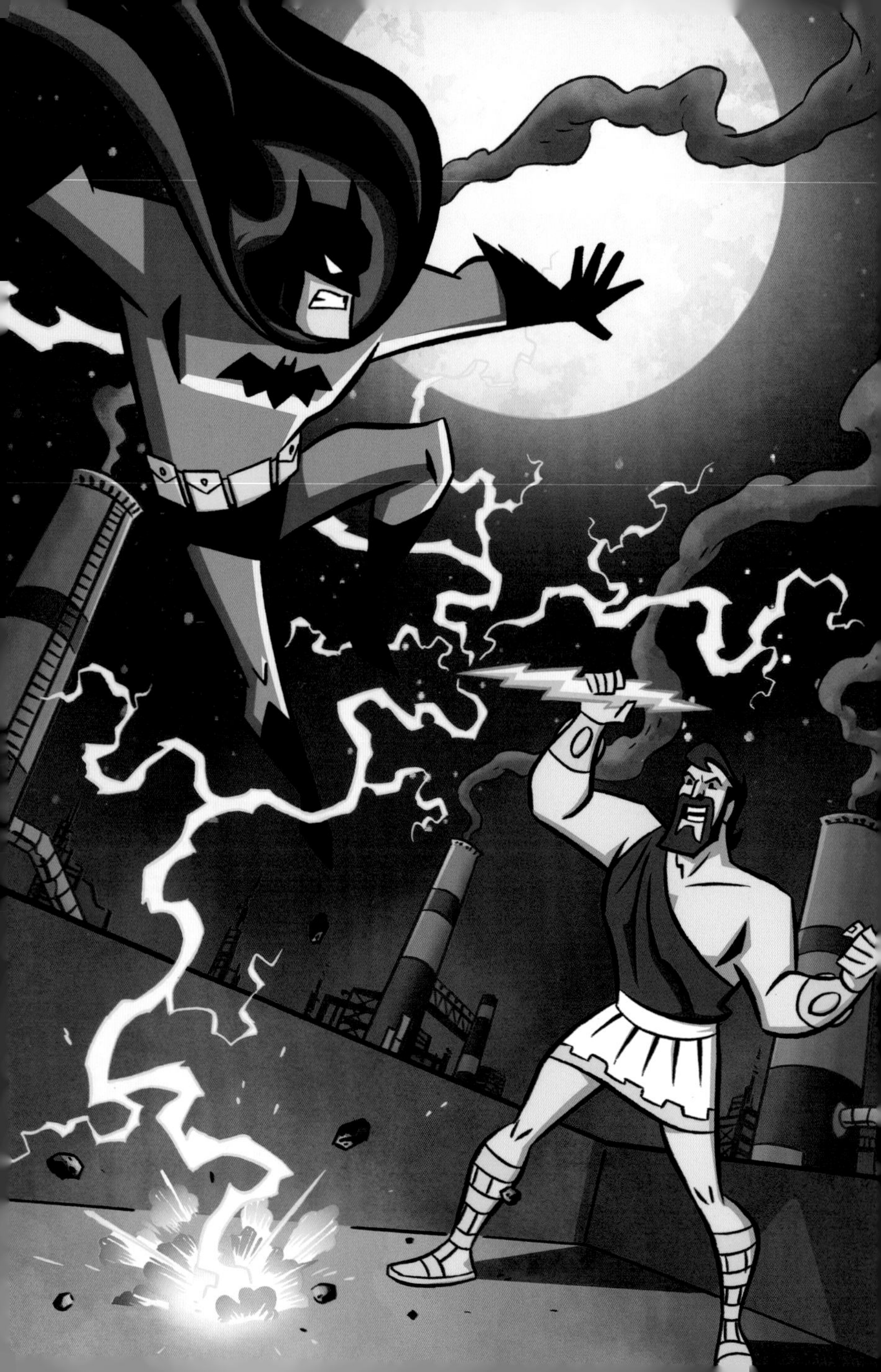

Zeus fires another bolt at Batman. ***ZZARK!*** It blasts the ground at Batman's feet, exploding the concrete around him.

BOOM! The Dark Knight is thrown off balance and lands on his back.

Maxie Zeus aims his weapon directly at Batman. "It's time to submit to your new king," Zeus says.

"No, it's time to fight fire with fire," Batman growls. He grabs a handheld stun gun from his Utility Belt. Batman activates the weapon and jams it against Zeus's ribs.

ZAP!

A powerful surge of energy sends Maxie Zeus sprawling across the roof. The maniacal madman doubles over in a smoldering heap.

Batman scans the area for the lightning rod. But it's nowhere to be found. He looks over the side of the building and peers into the darkness. *Hmm,* Batman thinks. *It couldn't just disappear. Perhaps it fell into the river.*

Turn the page.

Soon swirling red and blue lights and wailing sirens fill the air. Several police cruisers screech to a halt near the power plant.

Batman carries Zeus down to the waiting squad car of Detective Harvey Bullock. "You're under arrest, your lordship," Bullock barks at the villain.

Zeus is slightly conscious and mumbles, "I committed my crimes … at the behest of Chronos!"

"Sounds like something more sinister is at play," Batman says.

"Nah, this Greek freak is just spouting gibberish!" Bullock replies. He escorts Maxie Zeus into his waiting squad car.

As the cruiser drives away, Batman gets into the Batmobile and disappears into the night.

Moments later, Batman pulls into a dark alley. He changes out of his Batsuit and into an expensive tuxedo.

"Time to play the part of my alter-ego," Batman says to himself, "billionaire businessman Bruce Wayne!"

Bruce sets the Batmobile's autopilot to return to the Batcave. Then he straightens his tie and walks toward the Gotham City Museum of Art. The Egyptian Exhibit is hosting a private party for the unveiling of a rare new artifact.

A red carpet lines the front entrance. People are crammed on either side to see the glittering and glamorous Gotham City elite. As Bruce reaches the red carpet, a black town car drives up to the curb.

"Perfect timing, Alfred, as usual," Bruce says to the driver.

A proper English gentleman, Alfred Pennyworth is Bruce's loyal butler and closest friend. "I strive to impress you with my promptness, sir," Alfred replies drily.

The butler opens the passenger door of the car, and a strapping young man exits.

Turn the page.

"Dick Grayson, what a pleasant surprise," Bruce exclaims. "What brings you to Gotham City?"

"Alfred," Dick answers with a wink.

"Everyone's a comedian," Bruce replies.

Once an orphaned acrobat, Dick Grayson was adopted by Bruce Wayne as his youthful ward. Bruce trained the boy to become Batman's junior partner—Robin, the Boy Wonder!

After Dick graduated from college, he retired his cape and became Nightwing. He now works to protect the nearby city of Blüdhaven.

"Actually, sir, I took the liberty of contacting Master Grayson about the gala," Alfred explains. "A simple precaution in case your ... work ... kept you from attending."

"Prompt *and* prudent," remarks Bruce. "You deserve a raise."

"Now *you're* the comedian," Alfred retorts. The butler tips his hat and drives off in the car.

Bruce and Dick enter the museum amidst a flurry of camera flashes. They cross the grand foyer into the gallery of Greek statues. Standing there is a beautiful young redhead in a shimmering blue gown.

"You're fashionably late," she says.

"You know that's how I roll, Barbara," Dick says with a smirk.

"Hello, Ms. Gordon," Bruce says. "You look radiant, as usual."

Barbara Gordon is the daughter of Police Commissioner James Gordon. She is also secretly Batgirl, another crime fighter in Gotham City.

"Thanks, Bruce," Barbara replies. "I was just brushing up on my Greek mythology. It says here that Zeus has a very *electric* personality." She looks at Bruce with a twinkle in her eye.

Turn the page.

"That he does," the billionaire says grimly. "And dangerous, too."

"Speaking of Greek gods," purrs a woman's voice behind Bruce. "What's it take for a statue like you to crack a smile?"

Bruce turns to see Selina Kyle. The former socialite and famed cat burglar is decked out in a black dress and white diamonds.

"It's no laughing matter whenever *you* enter a museum, Ms. Kyle," Bruce states.

"Relax, darling," Selina purrs again. "I gave Catwoman the night off."

She takes Bruce by the arm. "Why don't we find out what all the fuss is about?"

The foursome walks into the Egyptian wing. Around them, the other guests excitedly discuss the unveiling of the museum's newest addition.

The group soon stands before the Temple of Isis. "This stone structure is the largest and most popular destination of the entire museum," Barbara says.

"You sound like you work here," Dick teases.

In the center of the temple stands a display case with a drape over it. Next to it, a smartly dressed curator quiets the guests.

"Welcome, ladies and gentlemen!" she announces. "You are about to witness history in the making. The oldest surviving document of ancient Egyptian history has just been discovered."

The crowd inches closer, buzzing with curiosity. Out of the corner of his eye, Bruce notices a woman walking in the opposite direction of the crowd. Her long brown hair hides half her face, but she looks very familiar. Bruce is unsettled by her presence. His instincts tell him that she's trouble.

"And without further ado," continues the curator, "I present to you … THE SCROLL OF ANUBIS!"

If Bruce follows the mystery woman, turn to page 18.
If Bruce stays and watches the ceremony, turn to page 28.

The mysterious woman walks out into the main hall.

Bruce excuses himself and pushes past the crowd toward the exit. By the time he reaches it, the woman is gone. Bruce closes his eyes and lets his other senses take over.

Bruce first catches a whiff of perfume. Then he hears the faint tapping of high heels coming from his left. Bruce enters the Grecian gallery filled with various relics made of gold and bronze.

Using a small tool kit from her purse, the woman has cut a hole into one of the display cases. Bruce finds her removing one of the priceless artifacts—a small statue of a Greek god.

"You know, they have a copy of that exact piece for sale in the gift shop," Bruce says. Startled, the woman whirls to face him.

Bruce is surprised. "Talia!" he exclaims.

"Greetings, my dear," she says. "I'd like to stay and talk, but I'm on a mission."

Bruce overcomes his shock and says, "Whatever it is, I can't allow you to complete it. Especially if it's for your father."

Talia is the daughter of Rā's al Ghūl, Batman's most powerful enemy. Rā's is said to be hundreds of years old. He has sustained his life by bathing in a mystical pool known as the Lazarus Pit.

His name translates to "Head of the Demon." Rā's is the leader of the Society of Shadows. This legion of followers wants to restore Earth's environment to its perfect state, without human influence.

"My father is a visionary," Talia tells Bruce. "Pity you don't see eye to eye with him. You're both very similar. You have the same intellect, strength, and determination."

Turn the page.

Rā's al Ghūl once offered the Dark Knight a place in the Society of Shadows as his successor. But Batman refused.

"I am nothing like your father. His vision is to destroy the human population," Bruce exclaims.

"It's a small price to pay for the perfect planet," shrugs the Daughter of the Demon.

Talia places the relic into her purse. "Good-bye," she says, blowing Bruce a kiss. "Until we meet again."

Talia starts for the exit but Bruce blocks her path. "This ends here, Talia," he says.

SKEEEESH!

"AIEEEEEEEEE!"

Suddenly, the sound of breaking glass and screams comes echoing from the main hall.

"Actually, it has only begun," Talia replies.

If Bruce stops Talia from stealing the artifact, go to page 21.
If Bruce rushes toward the screams, turn to page 41.

Talia turns to run away but Bruce grabs her arm. "How sweet," she says. "You want to hold my hand."

Talia quickly performs a judo throw, lifting Bruce off his feet and crashing him onto the floor.

WHUMP!

"Looks like you've fallen for me," Talia says with a laugh.

"How about I sweep you off your feet instead?" Bruce replies.

With a swift sweep kick, he knocks Talia off balance and she tumbles onto her back.

THUD!

The stolen artifact slips out of her hands and skitters across the polished marble floor.

Turn the page.

Bruce instantly jumps to his feet and races after the relic.

Talia gets up and rips off her gown to reveal a skintight purple suit beneath. She front flips past the billionaire to reach the relic first and scoops it up.

Bruce sprints toward her as she slinks behind a row of large bronze statues. "Come out, come out, wherever you are," Bruce says.

"I prefer to play hard to get," Talia calls out. She heaves a heavy statue of Herakles off of its pedestal so it falls toward Bruce ...

RRUMMBBLE!

If Bruce catches the priceless statue, turn to page 24.
If Bruce continues to chase Talia, turn to page 26.

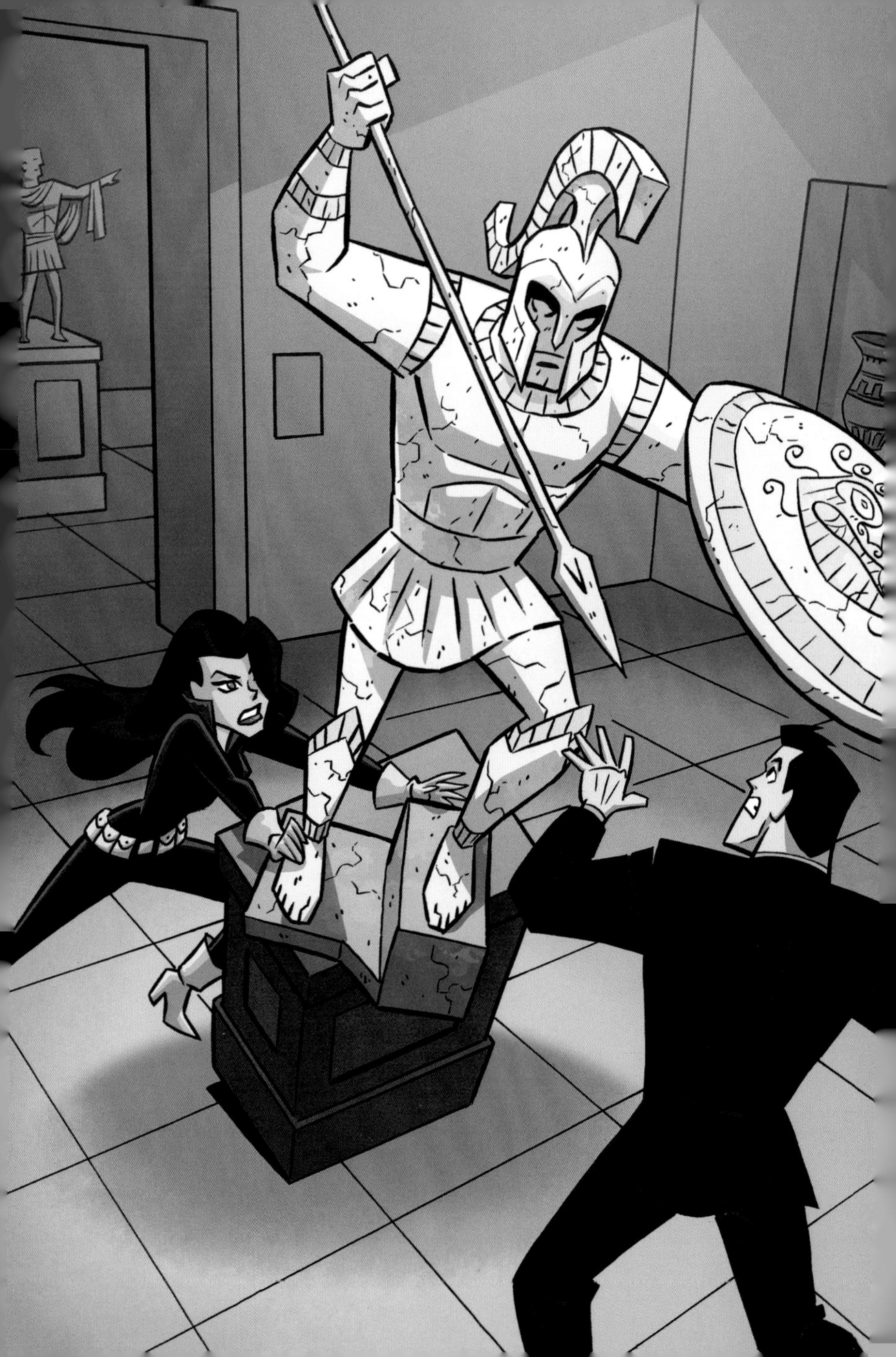

Bruce changes course and runs to the statue. He catches it on his shoulders and squats under its enormous weight.

WHUMP!

"You look like Atlas holding up the world," Talia taunts. "Sorry my departure is such a burden to you!"

Grunting and straining, Bruce straightens his legs and sets the Herakles statue right with all his might. The billionaire wipes his sweaty brow and breathes a sigh of relief.

Across the room, a rope ladder unfurls itself from an open skylight. Talia climbs onto it, and the ladder is pulled back up toward the ceiling. "The Society of Shadows rises again!" she yells.

As the thief makes her escape, she blows Bruce a kiss and waves good-bye.

"You're not the only one with a few tricks up their sleeve," Bruce says as he removes his tie clip.

The small device is really a Batarang in disguise! Bruce unfolds the small projectile and hurls it at his target.

SWISH!

It streaks through the air and slices the strap of Talia's bag. The bag tips over, dropping the artifact into Bruce's waiting hands.

"I'm doing an awful lot of catching today," he says.

Talia scowls. Her plot has been foiled. "Mark my words," she calls down. "This is only the beginning!" Then she is gone.

"Now that the Society of Shadows has returned, it's only a matter of time before they make their next move," Bruce says. "But I'll be ready to face them head on as Batman!"

THE END

To follow another path, turn to page 17.

Bruce chases Talia across the museum floor. She heads for the far end of the room directly below an open skylight.

A coiled rope ladder unfurls itself and cascades to the ground. Talia climbs onto it and is quickly lifted into the air. "Ciao for now!" she calls down.

Bruce takes a running leap and jumps on the ladder beneath Talia. But just as he grabs the ladder, Talia slices through the ropes with her bladed stiletto heel. *SWISH!*

Bruce plummets to the ground and braces himself for impact. His momentum causes him to roll across the shiny marble floor—right under the falling statue!

Bruce quickly jumps to his feet. He catches the heavy statue before it shatters into a thousand pieces.

Bruce bends his knees and looks like the Titan Atlas carrying the world on his back. Grunting loudly, he strains under the pressure.

Thanks to Talia, the billionaire is trapped between a rock and a hard place. "Looks like we're both in a tight spot," he says to Herakles.

Bruce watches Talia as she makes her escape. An evil grin spreads across her lips and she blows him a kiss.

Annoyed, Bruce manages to contact Dick with the remote communicator in his cufflink. Now he must wait for help ... and keep himself from getting crushed!

THE END

To follow another path, turn to page 17.

"The Scroll of Anubis is the oldest Egyptian document ever found," explains the curator. She pulls back the drape to reveal an incredibly old parchment with hieroglyphs painted across it.

"Anubis was the Egyptian god of the Underworld. He could grant the gift of life after death. Many have performed magic rituals in his honor in the hope of achieving eternal life."

People in the crowd inch closer so they can get a look at the parchment. Bruce, Dick, Barbara, and Selina are very impressed. Reporter Vicki Vale elbows her way to the front to snap a few pictures with her camera.

"Some say it contains ancient secrets of immortality," continues the curator. "These same scholars believe that the scroll is really a map that leads to the entrance of the Underworld itself!"

Suddenly, glass shatters from the skylight above.

SKRAASH!

A group of ninjas drop in on the startled crowd. The masked warriors scurry left and right, covering every corner of the temple. Some of the guests scream with fear. Others grip each other and huddle together.

Four ninjas leap to the middle of the room and surround the display case. They unsheathe their swords. *SHWING!*

Bruce exchanges looks with Dick and Barbara. "We need to end this situation fast," he whispers.

"With the exits blocked off, it won't be as Batman, Nightwing, and Batgirl," Dick replies. "Unless you want to give away our secret identities."

A serious man in colorful ceremonial robes emerges from the pack.

"Ladies and gentlemen, I am Rā's al Ghūl," he says. "I did not receive an invitation to this glamorous gathering. So it was necessary for me to, well, … *crash* the party!"

Turn the page.

Rā's glides toward the display case and throws back his long sleeves. The leader of the Society of Shadows caresses the glass gently.

"At long last," he says with an evil smile. "The Scroll of Anubis! One more piece of the puzzle to perfecting our planet."

Rā's unsheathes his long scimitar, the Serpent's Head, and smashes the glass case.

SKREESH!

With one swift movement, the villain removes the priceless papyrus and holds it triumphantly.

"The future begins now!" the Demon's Head exclaims, as the crowd gasps in horror.

Bruce clenches his jaw and prepares to make a move.

If Bruce confronts Rā's, turn to page 32.
If Bruce, Dick, and Barbara try to sneak out, turn to 36.

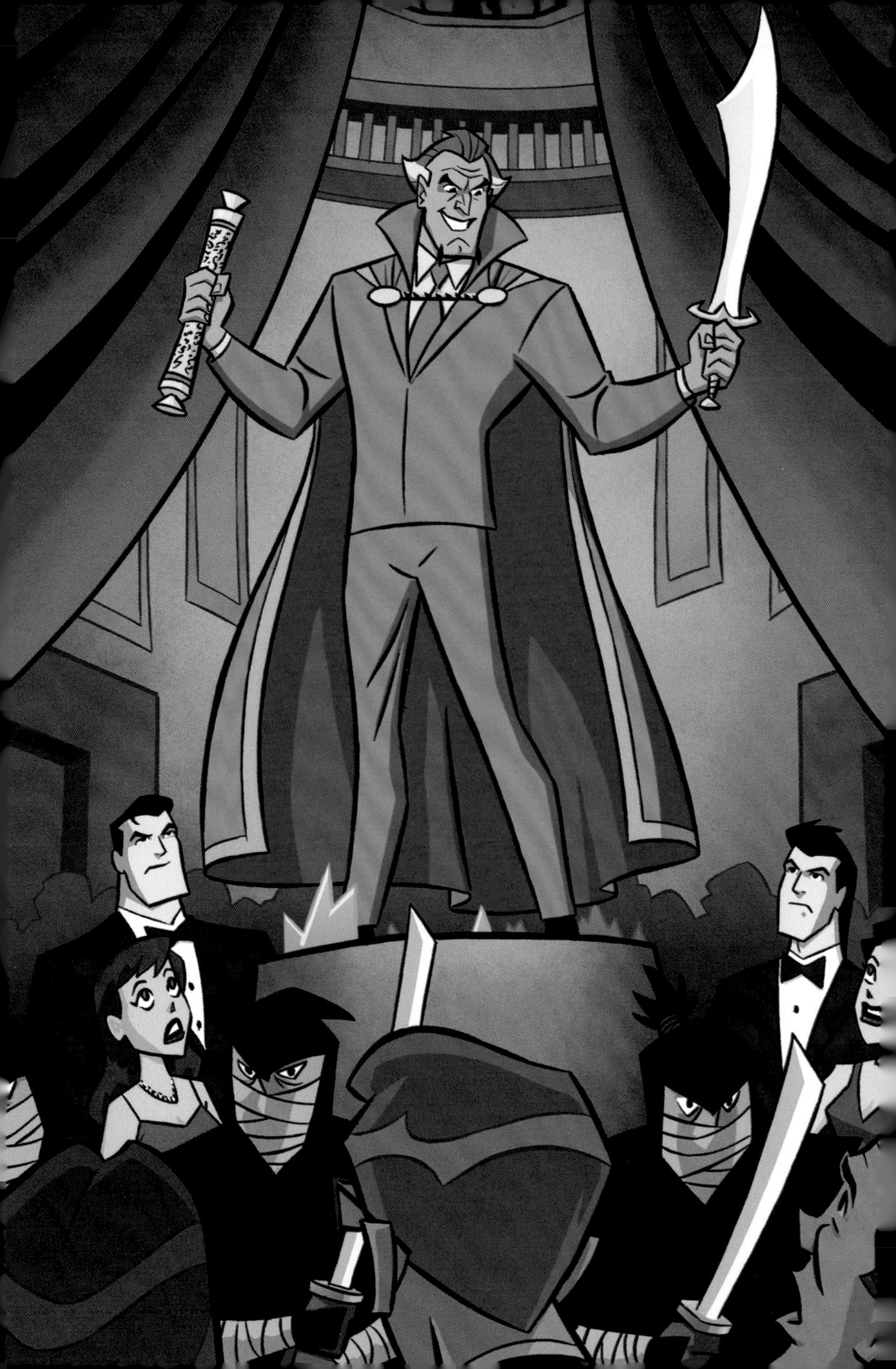

Bruce pushes through the crowd and confronts Rā's al Ghūl. "You better give that back," the billionaire says. "It belongs in the museum!"

He reaches for the leader of the Society of Shadows, but his path is blocked immediately.

CLANG!

Two of the ninja warriors cross their swords in front of Bruce. Their sharp blades glint under the museum lights.

"Well, if it isn't Bruce Wayne!" laughs Rā's. "A pleasure to see you again!" He removes the scroll from his robes and unfurls it gingerly.

"You rich people think you can take anything you want because of your money and power," Rā's says as he holds up the scroll. "Do you know what power this really holds?"

Bruce steps back, and the ninjas lower their swords.

"This is front page news!" Vicki Vale says and pulls out her smartphone. The journalist starts recording the events.

With blinding speed, a ninja leaps forward and slices the phone in half with his sword.

SLASH!

"Hey!" Vicki cries. "You'd better pay for that!"

The ninja advances toward the reporter, staring her down. Vicki stands her ground, but there is fear in her eyes.

Thinking quickly, Bruce uses the distraction to rush at the ninjas guarding Rā's al Ghūl. He pushes them to the ground and grabs Rā's by the lapels of his robe.

"Why don't your men pick on someone their own size?" he shouts.

"As you wish, Mr. Wayne," Rā's says coolly.

He waves his hand and the ninjas point their swords at Dick, Barbara, and Selina. "Now it's your move," Rā's replies with an evil grin.

Turn the page.

Bruce looks at his friends and then at the frightened guests. *This is not the best place to fight the Society of Shadows,* he thinks. There are too many innocent lives at stake. He lets go of Rā's.

The villain smooths his robes and gives a sly, knowing smile. "Smart man," he says.

Then he leans in and whispers, "You wouldn't want to give your true identity away in front of the guests, Detective." Rā's is one of the few people who knows that Bruce Wayne is really Batman, the World's Greatest Detective.

Bruce clenches his jaw and gives the madman a steely stare. "Until next time," the billionaire says.

"Indeed, old friend," Rā's replies.

He snaps his fingers, and one of the ninjas hurls a small gas pellet to the ground.

FSSSSSS!

A thick cloud of smoke fills the room. The museum patrons gag and cough. When the smoke clears, the Society of Shadows is gone!

The guests make their way to the exits, gasping for fresh air.

Bruce pulls Dick aside. "Very clever," he says. "Rā's used that smoke screen to escape. But he's not the only one with tricks up his sleeves."

"What do you mean?" asks Dick.

"When I grabbed his robe I placed a Bat-Tracker on him. He'll soon lead us to his final destination and we'll take him down."

"Awesome," Dick says. "So, what do we do next?"

"Nothing," says Bruce. "We've got a long night ahead of us. But we might as well enjoy the rest of the evening with these lovely ladies."

"It's a tough job, but somebody's gotta do it," Dick says with a smile.

THE END

To follow another path, turn to page 17.

While Rā's al Ghūl addresses his captive audience, Bruce, Dick, and Barbara calmly walk toward the back of the room.

"Those ninjas don't know this museum like I do," Bruce whispers. "This hidden door leads back to the main hall." Bruce turns the knob and the trio disappears behind the door.

Once outside, Barbara parts ways with her friends. "I'll catch up with you later," she says. "There's something I need to do."

Bruce and Dick run to a nearby alley where Alfred waits for them in the car. "To the Batcave!" Bruce says, as they speed out of the city toward Wayne Manor.

Meanwhile, Selina is entranced by the Society of Shadows. When she finally turns away, she sees that the others are long gone.

"Hmph! They must have run off at the first sign of trouble. Such scaredy-cats," she mutters to herself. "It's time Catwoman took matters into her own claws!" She then slinks through the crowd to find another exit.

Back at the Batcave, Bruce and Dick change into Batman and Nightwing. Batman goes to the Batcomputer and taps into the security cameras at the museum. Scanning the footage, the Dynamic Duo discover that three items were stolen!

"Rā's wasn't the only thief tonight. In addition to stealing the Scroll of Anubis, the video shows his daughter Talia stealing an artifact from the Grecian wing. His servant Ubu robbed the Peruvian wing too," Batman says.

"Each item must play a part in their sinister scheme," Nightwing replies.

"But what is the Society of Shadows up to?" Alfred asks.

VROOOOM!

Suddenly, a caped figure drives a motorcycle into the Batcave. The driver removes her helmet to reveal the masked face of Batgirl!

Turn the page.

"Now who's fashionably late?" Nightwing says with a smile.

Batgirl parks her Batcycle and walks over to her partners. She removes a small flash drive from her Utility Belt. "I had to check out a few things from the library," she replies.

"The library? How quaint," Nightwing quips. "We have a Batcomputer, you know."

Batgirl rolls her eyes. "Is that so? I doubt your high-tech machine could track down the complete Scroll of Anubis. It doesn't exist online."

Batgirl shows Nightwing her library card. "My method was much more low-tech. See? The library has an entire archive of ancient documents. I snapped a few photos and loaded them on here for you." She hands the flash drive to Batman.

Turn the page.

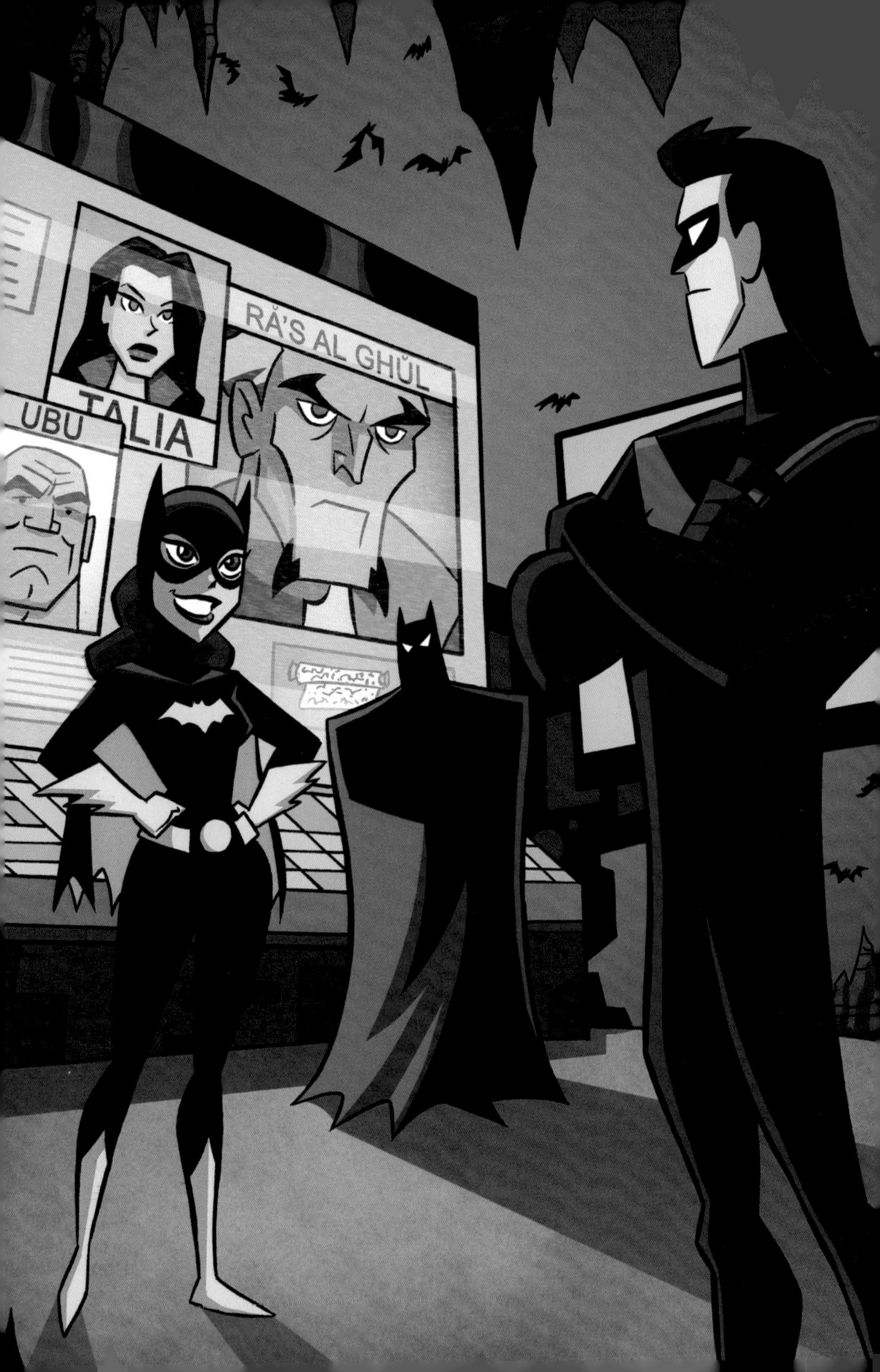
TALIA
RĂ'S AL GHŬL
UBU

"If the Scroll of Anubis really is an ancient map to the Underworld, the Society of Shadows will stop at nothing to find it," Batgirl says.

"And Rā's al Ghūl was likely around when the rituals for eternal life were originally performed," adds Nightwing.

"My hunch is you're both correct," Batman says. "Rā's al Ghūl is probably hunting for another Lazarus Pit to renew his body. Those relics are probably each an important part of the puzzle. His ultimate quest is to control Death itself!"

"Spooky," Batgirl replies. "Looks like we've got a long road ahead of us."

"Indeed," Batman says. "I plan to follow the relics and find out what Rā's is up to. Lucky for us, the museum's artifacts are all tagged with a hidden tracker. We can use the Batcomputer to find the signals. If we can find them, then we can figure out what the Society of Shadows is after."

If the heroes follow the clues to Greece, turn to page 50.
If they track the villains to Peru, turn to page 69.
If they try to find Rā's al Ghul in Egypt, turn to page 89.

Bruce rushes out into the main hall. *The screams are coming from the Temple of Isis,* he thinks.

Suddenly, a dark figure slinking in the South American wing catches Bruce's eye. The billionaire enters the dimly lit gallery instead.

The room appears to be empty, except for the three rows of glass display cases. They contain figurines and pottery made of stone and clay.

CRACK! SMASH!

Bruce races toward the noise and nearly collides with a speeding shadow. The billionaire catches the mystery person in a vice-like hold.

"Mee-ouch!" cries a familiar voice. "Ease up on the kung-fu grip!"

"Selina!" Bruce exclaims in shock. "What are you doing in here?"

Turn the page.

"Do you know who else has an annoying habit of jumping out of nowhere?" Selina asks, rubbing her wrist. "The big bad Batman. You two are a lot alike now that I think of it ..."

"Up to your old tricks?" Bruce asks, changing the subject. "What did you steal this time?" He points to a little stone statue in her hand.

"Relax, Moneybags," Selina snaps back. "This isn't a robbery. It's a hit and run."

"I beg your pardon?" asks Bruce.

At that moment, a hulking brute emerges from the shadows rubbing his bald head. He's wearing a tight vest and baggy harem pants.

Bruce recognizes the man. It's Ubu, the dangerous and deadly servant of Rā's al Ghūl!

"That guy was trying to steal this statue," Selina explains. "So I hit him on the head with a heavy pot and ran."

Ubu trudges forward, staring down Bruce with a fierce look.

"So we meet again, infidel," Ubu sneers. "I hope it will be for the last time!"

The bulky bodyguard has a personal grudge against the Golden Boy of Gotham City. There was a time when Rā's wanted Ubu as his successor to lead the Society of Shadows. Then Rā's met Batman and changed his mind.

Ubu lifts a large stone relic off a pedestal and crumbles it with his bare hands. He sprinkles the dust on the floor and points to Bruce.

"That is what I am going to do to you," Ubu snarls.

Selina gasps. Bruce needs to act fast.

If Bruce fights Ubu, turn to page 44.
If he and Selina run, turn to page 47.

Bruce positions himself between Selina and their oncoming attacker. "Stand down," he tells Ubu. "Don't make me hurt you."

Ubu laughs and puts up his fists, taking a fighter's stance. Bruce does the same.

"You're not seriously going to fight this guy?" Selina says, trying to pull Bruce back. "He's as big as a mountain!"

Ubu roars and charges at Bruce, tackling him to the ground. *WHUMP!*

The two men wrestle, slipping and sliding across the polished marble floor. Bruce lands a few quick jabs on Ubu's jaw, but they barely slow him down.

The bodyguard headbutts the billionaire and comes out on top.

CRACK!

Ubu pins Bruce down and gets ready to rearrange his face. "Say good-bye to your good looks, Pretty Boy!" Ubu yells.

Turn the page.

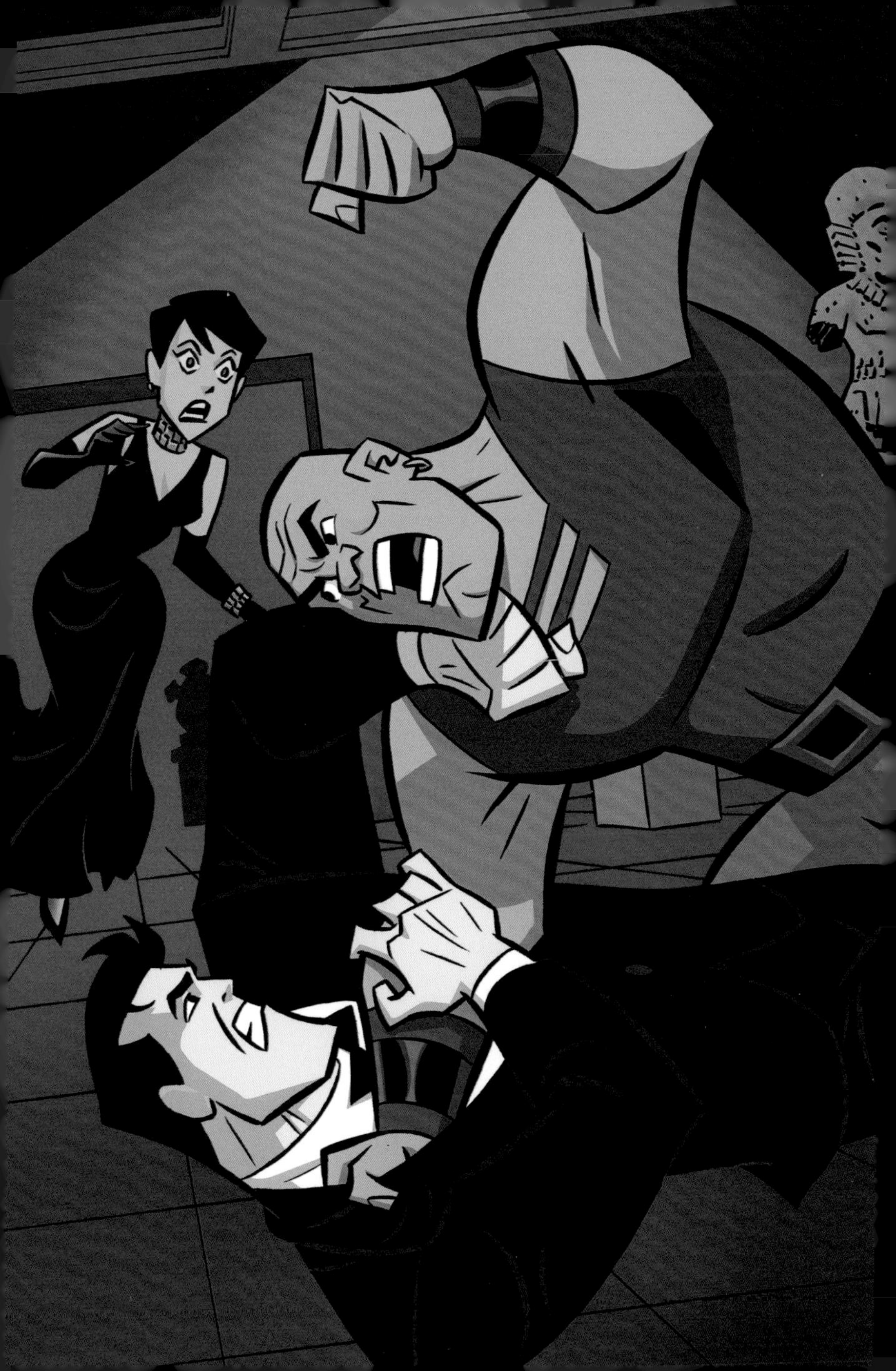

Selina picks up a large clay pot and sneaks behind Ubu. "Here we go again!" she shouts, and brings the heavy object down hard over Ubu's head.

CRACK! The monster-sized menace grunts and tips over sideways.

Selina helps Bruce up. "You should stick to picking up the check instead of picking fights," she jokes.

But then Ubu gets back on his feet. He quickly grabs the small statue from where Selina dropped it. Then he pulls out a smoke pellet and throws it down.

FSSSSSSSSSSSSS! A thick cloud of smoke fills the air. "The Society of Shadows will rise!" Ubu shouts as he makes his escape.

Bruce and Selina cough and gag as Ubu's knockout gas overwhelms them. When the smoke clears, the two of them lay unconscious on the floor—and Ubu is long gone.

THE END

To follow another path, turn to page 17.

Ubu snarls and lunges at Bruce. The billionaire nimbly moves aside and trips the charging mountain of muscle.

THUD!

Ubu slides across the polished marble floor. Bruce grabs Selina by the hand and the duo dash into the main hall.

"What was that all about?" Selina asks.

"It's a long story," Bruce replies. "I thought it was all ancient history."

Selina clutches the small idol as Bruce leads her toward the Egyptian wing. There they find Dick and Barbara watching the shocking commotion that began only minutes ago.

A band of ninjas swarms the room, threatening the guests with their swords. One of them snatches the cover away from the display case to reveal the Scroll of Anubis.

The crowd gasps as a serious man in colorful robes enters the room.

Turn the page.

"Ladies and gentlemen, I am Rā's al Ghūl," he says. "Please forgive the interruption. But as I did not receive an invitation, I had little choice but to crash this lovely party!"

Rā's approaches the display case and caresses the glass gently. "Finally," he says with an evil smile, "the Scroll of Anubis! The prize I've long sought to perfect our planet."

Rā's pulls out his scimitar, the Serpent's Head, and smashes the glass case.

SKREESH!

The villain quickly removes the priceless artifact and carefully tucks it into his robe.

"The future has arrived!" Rā's exclaims.

The curator gasps in horror. "What's going on?" she cries.

Rā's snaps his fingers and the ninjas point their swords at the guests. Everyone in the room is now a hostage.

"Enjoy the rest of your evening," Rā's cackles. "I know I will." Just as quickly as he arrived, the Demon's Head makes his exit.

"Rā's al Ghūl is up to one of his ghoulish schemes of global domination," Bruce whispers to Dick. "The scroll and the idol are two pieces of a complex puzzle that raises more questions than answers."

"There's nothing we can do about it now without giving away our identities," Dick replies. "We'll have to regroup later after the police arrive."

Bruce nods his head, but grits his teeth in frustration. "By that time, Rā's will have disappeared to the far corners of the globe," he says grimly. "Along with any hopes of catching him!"

THE END

To follow another path, turn to page 17.

"First, let's take a closer look at the museum's security footage," Batman says as he zooms in on the image. "Look, that's Talia in the Grecian wing. She's stealing a small statue and a handful of coins. The museum directory says that the statue was of the god Thanatos. The coins were Charon's Obols."

"Thanatos was the Greek god of Death," Nightwing explains. "Charon's Obols were coins the ancient Greeks buried with the dead. They were supposedly used to pay ferryman, Charon. He brought people's souls across the river Styx to enter the Underworld."

"I'm impressed," says Batgirl.

"I've studied Greek myths for years," Nightwing says with a smile. "The Underworld is ruled by the god Hades. It's also guarded by Cerberus, a giant three-headed dog!"

"Well, now you're just showing off," Batgirl replies. "Does Rā's al Ghūl plan on taking a ferryboat ride to the Underworld?"

BEEP! BEEP! BEEP!

"The Society of Shadows is on the move," Batman says pointing at a radar screen. "This light shows that Talia and the artifact are headed for Greece. Nightwing, you know this subject well. I'd like you to join me in tracking her down."

Nightwing nods in agreement and heads off to ready the Batplane with gear and supplies.

"Batgirl, I need you to monitor the activity of the other missing relics and keep us updated," Batman continues.

"Aye, aye, Captain," Batgirl says with a salute. "Safe travels!"

Batman enters the Batplane and punches in the coordinates for Chios, an island in the Aegean Sea. Within minutes, the sleek black plane is speeding across the Atlantic Ocean.

ZOOOOOOM!

Turn the page.

A few hours later, the aircraft touches down on a mountaintop in the village of Anavatos. It is almost dawn when the heroes climb silently down the craggy terrain.

Batman spies a man creeping between the trees and grabs him. "Who are you?" Batman asks.

"Please don't hurt me!" cries the man. "My name is Nikos Drossos, and I'm a goat herder." Just then, a handful of goats gallop by.

CLOP! CLOP! CLOP!

"Apologies, sir," Nightwing says. "But we're looking for the Temple of Hades."

"Are you g-g-ghosts?" Mr. Drossos asks, trembling.

"Something like that," Nightwing replies.

The man looks at the Dynamic Duo and scratches his head. "You must go into the town square. You will find the temple there."

"Thank you," Nightwing says. Then he and Batman dash off into the darkness.

The village of Anavatos is a medieval settlement of stone houses built into the side of the mountain. It is rocky and steep, but the heroes continue their climb without breaking a sweat.

"That poor man probably thought you were the boogeyman," Nightwing says to Batman.

"Anavatos is a literal ghost town," Batman states.

"Do you mean that it's been abandoned ... or that it's haunted by spooks?" Nightwing asks.

"Neither will surprise me," Batman says with a slight grin. "So let's find out."

If Batman and Nightwing investigate the streets, turn to page 54.

If they climb onto the rooftops, turn to page 56.

The Dynamic Duo sprint down the main street toward the town square. Aside from the shepherd and his flock, there's no other activity in the tiny village. Upon reaching their destination, Batman scans the area.

"The buildings are in disrepair and unused," he observes. "However, there's a section in the center of the square where the ground seems polished. It looks like it was recently disturbed."

Batman stands over the area and takes out the portable Batcomputer in his Utility Belt. He pulls up a 3-D holographic image of the Temple of Hades.

"Notice how the design on this granite slab matches that of the aerial layout of the temple," he says.

"It does," Nightwing replies. "There's a small groove here at the edge that shows where the entrance would be. Perhaps it's a keyhole?"

Suddenly, Nightwing's eyes light up and he snaps his fingers. "What if the relic stolen from the museum is the key!?"

"Great minds think alike, my friend," Batman says. "I had a hunch, so I created a model of the relic using the Batcave's 3-D printer."

Batman produces the copy of the small statue from another pouch in his Utility Belt.

Nightwing whistles. "No wonder they call you the World's Greatest Detective!"

Batman slides the copy of the relic into the groove. It's a perfect fit!

CREEEAAAK! FWSSSSSH! The stone creaks and lifts out of place. A secret hidden staircase leads underground.

"Do you think it's the entrance to the Underworld?" Nightwing asks.

"Most likely it's an entrance to the Society of Shadows criminal underworld … not the realm of the dead," Batman replies.

The heroes descend the dark steps and come upon two tunnels. The one on the left has a faint glow coming from it. The one on the right is pitch black.

If the heroes go left, turn to page 61.
If they go right, turn to page 64.

Batman and Nightwing take out their grapnel guns and use them to swing across the rooftops of the village.

"Everything seems quiet," says Nightwing.

All of a sudden … **FWIP! FWIP!** Something slices through the cables holding the heroes! Batman and Nightwing plummet and crash onto a ceramic shingle rooftop.

The hapless heroes slide down the slanted surface to a stone balcony below.

"What just happened?!" Nightwing asks, surprised. He dusts himself off and helps Batman to his feet.

"Only the sharpest bladed weapons can slice through our cables," Batman states.

SHUNK! SHUNK! Two razor-sharp shuriken pierce the ground at their feet.

Batman recognizes the throwing stars immediately. "The kind of weapons used by the Society of Shadows," adds the Dark Knight.

Just then, a swarm of black-clothed ninjas appears! "*HYAAAAAAAAH!*"

Batman and Nightwing are surrounded. The small balcony is crammed with bodies. "These guys are invading our personal space," Nightwing quips. "I say we kick them out!"

Batman grabs Nightwing and lifts him off the ground. Nightwing delivers a powerful double-kick and sends a group of ninjas toppling off the balcony.

Nightwing then somersaults onto the next balcony. Some of the fearsome foes follow him while Batman faces an army of attackers.

The Caped Crusader uppercuts the leading ninja—slamming him into another!

POW! THUD!

Batman senses more enemies sneaking up behind him. The Dark Knight performs a lightning-fast roundhouse kick ... sending all the ninjas sprawling off the balcony.

WHAP! BAM! CRACK!

Turn the page.

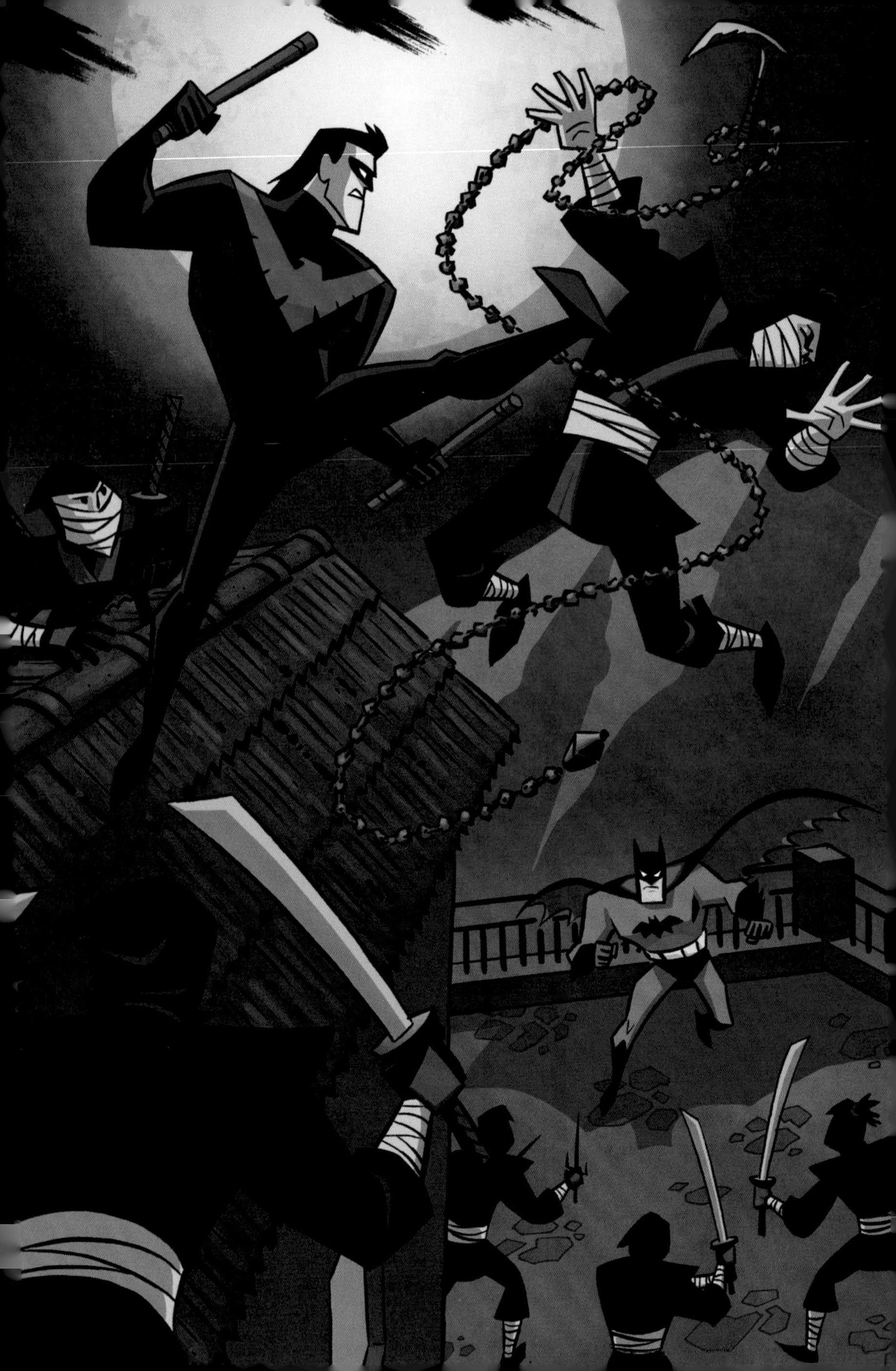

On the neighboring rooftop, Nightwing continues to fight with his trusty bo staffs. "Batter up!" Nightwing sings. "It's time to play ball!"

SMACK! WHACK! The ninjas flail their arms as they fall off the roof.

"HOMERUN!" Nightwing shouts.

But his happy grin turns sour when a second wave of warriors appears. "Looks like we've got a double header, Batman," he says.

Batman reaches into his Utility Belt and produces a handful of smoke pellets. He throws them at his feet, and a thick cloud of gas fills the air.

FSSSSSSSSS!

Within seconds, all but one of the ninjas have been sent to dreamland by the sleeping gas.

The Dark Knight grabs a foggy-headed foe. "Where is Rā's al Ghūl? Is he in Greece?" Batman demands. "Is he in Peru? Or Egypt?"

Turn the page.

The ninja stares at the Caped Crusader with glassy eyes and starts to laugh maniacally. "The Society of Shadows IS in Greece ... AND in Egypt ... AND Peru! We are everywhere ... and nowhere! Hahahaha!"

Within seconds, his body begins to smoke and disintegrate right in Batman's grasp!

SSSSSS-POOF! There is a puff of smoke and the heroes find that nothing remains of the ninja but his black robes.

Suddenly, the other ninjas start to disintegrate too. ***POOF! POOF! POOF!***

Once again, Batman and Nightwing are alone, but with more questions than answers.

"This dead end is only the beginning," Batman says. "We'll need to go back to the Batcave and follow other leads."

"Sounds like a plan," replies Nightwing. "Sooner or later, we'll smoke out Rā's al Ghūl!"

THE END

To follow another path, turn to page 17.

Batman and Nightwing follow the mysterious glow into a large cavern. In the center is a stone altar, surrounded by lit candles. A figure in a long black robe stands next to the altar, holding a tiny statue.

"I do hope we're interrupting something, Talia," Batman says.

The woman whirls to face the Caped Crusader. Her scowl transforms into an evil smile.

"Actually, we've been expecting you," she says. "This ritual requires the sacrifice of a living soul for a dead one to return. Thank you for bringing this one to me, Batman."

Suddenly, a tranquilizer dart whizzes at Nightwing and hits him in the shoulder. The drug acts quickly, and the woozy hero falls to his knees.

A handful of ninjas grab Nightwing and drag him toward the altar. "Hey!" he mumbles. "Get your mitts off me!"

Batman moves to stop them, but he is also grabbed by a number of strong hands.

Turn the page.

Talia draws close to Batman. "My father considers you his equal," she says. "Your presence here means you must have a copy of the key."

Talia removes Batman's Utility Belt. She reaches into a compartment and pulls out the duplicate statue.

"The Society of Shadows has eyes and ears everywhere. You must know that we can anticipate your every move," the Daughter of the Demon tells Batman.

As Talia walks away, Batman wrestles his hands free from his captors. He taps a hidden switch on his gauntlet. *CLICK!*

The fake relic ignites, detonating a hidden flash bomb within! *FWOOM!*

Thanks to their masks, Batman and Nightwing are protected from the intense burst of light. But Talia and her henchmen are temporarily blinded. They reach for their eyes and howl in pain.

"Bet you didn't see *that* coming," Batman says.

Batman takes out the ninjas surrounding him with a flurry of punches and kicks. Then he snatches his Utility Belt from Talia's clutches.

The Dark Knight rushes toward his partner and injects him with an antidote. In a few moments, Nightwing shakes off the toxin.

"It's payback time, boys!" Nightwing laughs. He grabs his captors and knocks their heads together. **_CLUNK!_**

Talia runs toward the exit. But before she can escape, Batman slaps the Bat-cuffs on her wrists.

"If your vision is still blurry, allow me to guide you back to Gotham City," he says. "Straight to a cell at Blackgate Penitentiary."

"You cannot stop the Society of Shadows," says Talia. "We will fulfill the destiny of Rā's al Ghūl!"

"Your father must be very proud," Nightwing replies. "And when he comes to visit you in prison, we'll have a nice cell waiting for him too!"

THE END

To follow another path, turn to page 17.

Batman and Nightwing take the dark path. The Caped Crusader lights a flare, filling the tunnel with a bright red glow. Enormous scorpions skitter across the floor.

SKRIT! SKRIT! SKRIT!

"I think we were better off walking in the dark," Nightwing says.

Batman uses the flare to inspect the passage. "The Society of Shadows is performing their secret rituals down here," he states. "I can smell burning incense."

"I think I hear voices too," Nightwing says.

SNAP! The young hero steps on a trip wire. "Uh, oh," he says. "That's bad, right?"

Suddenly, the floor drops out from under the heroes. Batman and Nightwing slide down a chute and land in a shallow pit of snakes!

HISSSSS! The serpents slither toward them, hungrily flicking their tongues and flashing their fangs. Nightwing kicks sand at the reptiles, causing them to recoil.

"Ah, Detective!" booms a loud voice. "How nice of you to drop in!"

The heroes turn to see Rā's al Ghūl emerging from a shimmering pool of glowing green liquid. Ubu and a small group of ninjas surround him.

"We have found a Lazarus Pit to restore me!" Rā's continues. "I'll use my newfound power to open a portal to the Underworld, overthrow Hades, and become ruler myself!"

"You're mad, Rā's!" Batman yells.

"Perhaps," Rā's replies. "But you're about to become a two-course meal!"

The ravenous reptiles slither closer to Batman and Nightwing. *HISSSSSSSSS!*

Thinking quickly, Batman grabs some liquid nitrogen pellets from his Utility Belt. He throws them at the snakes—freezing them in their tracks! *FWOOSH!*

"I'm amused by your ingenuity," Rā's tells the heroes.

Turn the page.

"In Greek mythology, you'll know that Hades' brother Zeus was the lord of lightning," Rā's continues. "Luckily, we came across an electrifying item from Zeus himself that will open the portal."

Ubu hands Rā's a large metal weapon. Batman recognizes it immediately—it's the lightning rod of Maxie Zeus!

Rā's activates the rod. It crackles with electricity. Then he slams it against the ground. The cavern rumbles, and the ground cracks open wide. Swirling mists and vapors rise up out of the opening.

Suddenly, the souls of the dead rise into the air! Their terrifying moans and howls echo off the walls.

YEEEAAAAOOOOOOH!

The frightening spirits extend their bony arms through tattered robes, reaching for the ninjas. "Run for your lives!" one of them yells.

Batman and Nightwing swing out of the snake pit on their Batropes. They rush at Rā's, but Ubu blocks their path.

The massive bodyguard swings at Batman, but the Dark Knight ducks. *SWISH!*

"Strike one!" Nightwing shouts.

Ubu swings at Nightwing who also ducks. *SWISH!* "Strike two!" Nightwing shouts again.

Ubu swings both his fists at the heroes but misses again. "And that's strike three!" Nightwing shouts.

Batman grabs Ubu and hurls him across the room into the snake pit. *WHUMP!* "You're out," Batman growls.

The heroes run toward Rā's al Ghūl. The villain is glowing with energy as the spirits swirl around him. "My loyal subjects!" he cries. "I am your new leader!"

But the ghosts don't want a leader. They begin to suck out his life force! "Stop!" he commands. "You can't do this to me!" His skin grows pale and wrinkled. And his hair turns gray.

"NOOOOO!" Rā's screams and drops the lightning rod to the ground.

Turn the page.

Batman picks up the weapon and hurls it into the chasm. **KRA-KOOM!** In a blinding flash, the ghosts are blasted back to the Underworld. Then, as quickly as it had opened, the cavern floor seals shut.

The Dark Knight leans down next to Rā's. The madman is still alive, but very weak and frail. "This is only a minor setback," rasps Rā's. "I will succeed next time."

The two heroes round up Rā's and Ubu. They lead the defeated villains back to the Batplane for the long flight back to Gotham City.

"Maxie Zeus mentioned he was working for Chronos, the Greek god of Time," Batman says. "I'm guessing that he meant you."

"Indeed," replies Rā's al Ghūl. "Time is one thing I have in abundance, Detective."

"Good," replies Nightwing. "Because you'll be spending a lot of it in Arkham Asylum."

THE END

To follow another path, turn to page 17.

"A stone idol of Supay, the Peruvian god of Death, was also stolen from the museum. That must be what Ubu took," Batgirl states.

Batman and Nightwing turn to her. Nightwing smiles. "More late-night studying at the library?"

"Real-world experience," Batgirl replies. "Studying abroad in South America. I also climbed Macchu Picchu to see the lost city of the Incas."

"Well, you got me there," Nightwing says.

BEEP! BEEP! BEEP!

"The Society of Shadows is on the move," Batman says pointing at a radar screen. "The idol is headed for Peru. Batgirl will join me on this mission, given her experience." She nods in agreement and heads off to prepare the Batplane.

"Nightwing, you'll monitor the activity of the other missing relics and keep us updated," Batman continues.

"Roger that," Nightwing says. "Safe travels!"

Turn the page.

Batman climbs up to join Batgirl in the Batplane's cockpit. He types in their coordinates and fires the plane's powerful thrusters.

SHOOM!

Within minutes, the sleek black Batplane is speeding toward the city of Cuzco in Peru.

"The mountain is located right above the Sacred Valley," Batgirl says. "The Incas built an entire estate on top of it in the 1400s. It's been abandoned for hundreds of years. Do you really think there's an active Lazarus Pit in the area?"

"There must be. Otherwise the Society of Shadows wouldn't have resurfaced," Batman replies grimly. "And Rā's al Ghūl will stop at nothing to quench his thirst for ultimate power."

"That stone idol represents the Underworld," Batgirl adds. "It could be a key to a hidden door."

"Let's go knock on it," the Dark Knight says.

A few hours later, the Batplane touches down on the mountaintop directly across from Machu Picchu. It's almost dawn.

"Even in stealth mode, the Batplane could be detected by the Society of Shadows," Batman says. "It's best to keep our distance."

Batgirl looks at the radar screen. "The tracking signal for the relic seems to be coming from inside the mountain!"

"We'd better move fast," Batman says.

The heroes exit the plane and reach a chasm at the edge of the mountain.

"Which way do we go?" Batgirl asks.

"We have two options," Batman answers. "We can cross here and sneak into the top of the ruins. Or, we can drop down into the jungle below and enter at the bottom."

If Batman and Batgirl climb the mountain, turn to page 72.
If the heroes go down into the jungle, turn to page 86.

"Let's take it from the top!" Batgirl exclaims.

The duo aim and shoot their grapnel guns, then swing across the chasm. ***WHOOOSH!*** At the last second, they spread their capes for a soft and silent landing on Machu Picchu.

The crime-fighters sneak along the outer walls of the temple and enter it cautiously. The space is quiet and empty. Wild grass has grown through the cracks in the floor.

"Look!" Batgirl says, pointing at the ground. "There's a faint green light shining up through the cracks in this stone."

"The Lazarus Pit is directly beneath us," Batman replies. "Rā's and all his minions must be down there right now."

"Not all of them," says a deep voice from the shadows.

Suddenly, Batgirl and Batman are seized by several black robed ninjas. A big hulking figure approaches them and strikes a match.

"Ubu," Batman growls.

"Bring them below!" Ubu commands.

The ninjas drag the heroes out of the temple and down a secluded path. At the end sits a large stone wall. It has a small groove in the middle. Ubu produces the stolen relic from his belt and places it into the groove.

RRRMMMBBLE, CHNK!

The statue of Supay slowly turns upside down. The wall slides away to reveal a hidden entrance.

"Told you so," Batgirl whispers.

The duo is dragged into a vast chamber. "Ah, Detective!" booms a loud voice.

The heroes turn to see Rā's al Ghūl emerging from a shimmering pool of glowing green liquid.

"The Lazarus Pit!" Batgirl exclaims.

"Indeed, young lady," Rā's bellows. "Now that I've completed my renewal ritual, I shall resurrect my newest army from the dead!"

If Batman and Batgirl watch the ritual, turn to page 74.
If the heroes rush to stop Rā's, turn to page 79.

Ubu hands the statue to Rā's al Ghūl and it begins to glow.

"Yes! I can feel it!" Rā's exclaims. "Such incredible power!"

Beams of light shoot from the statue and streak across the cavern. **FWOOOOSH!**

The walls rumble and shake. Rā's rises into the air and begins chanting an ancient spell. His voice echoes throughout the chamber.

Suddenly the ground cracks open at Ubu's feet, causing him to fall in! He grabs onto the edge and hangs on for dear life.

"What's happening?" Batgirl asks.

"It's the beginning of the end!" cries Rā's.

Seconds later, dead and decaying Incan warriors begin climbing out of the pit. They raise their weapons and charge at once.

"**RARRRRRR!**" they shout. The ninja fighters flee in terror at the sight of the zombies.

Turn the page.

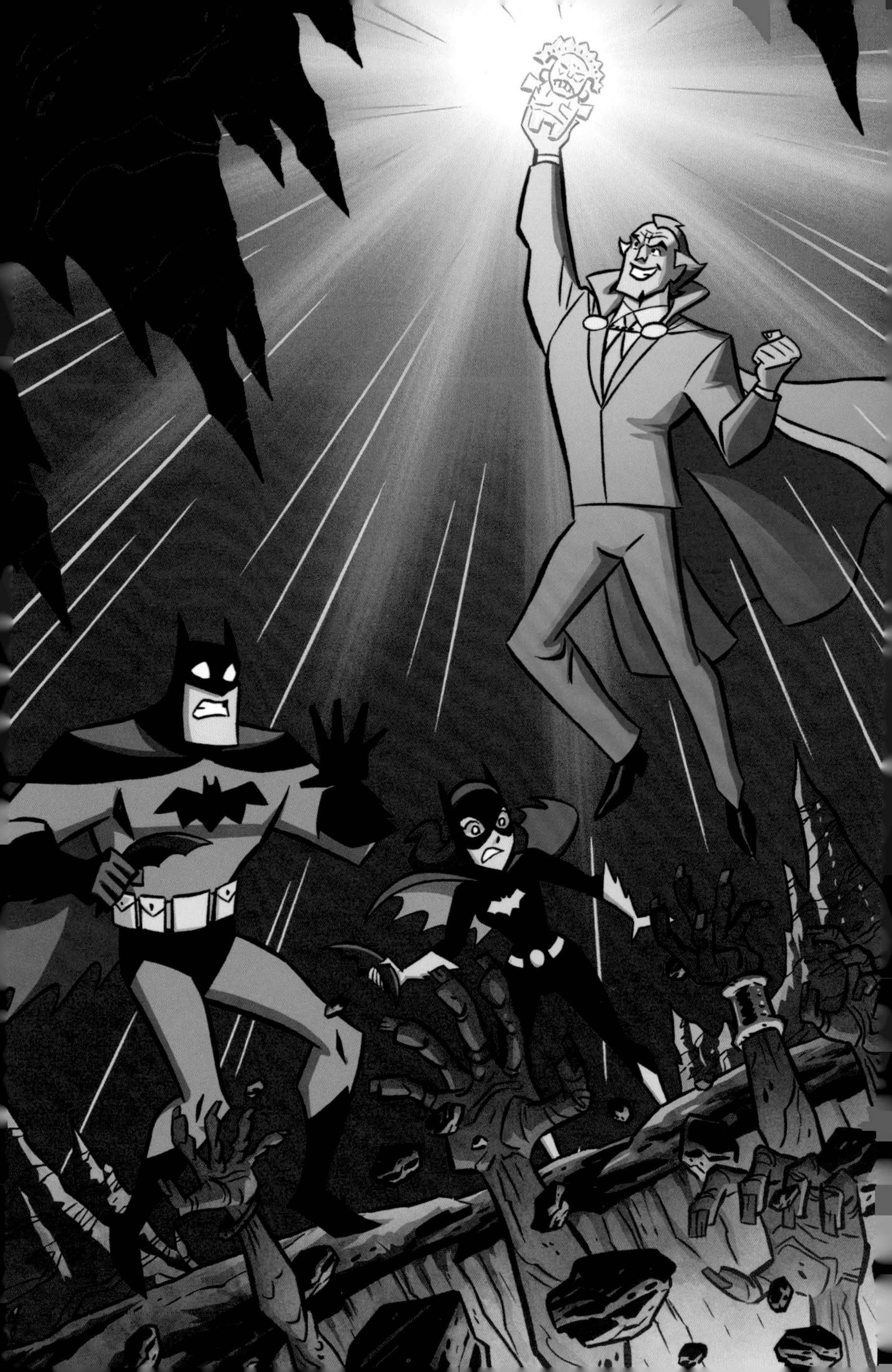

"**RARRRRRR!**" the undead warriors shout again as they close in on Batman and Batgirl. The heroes hurl Batarangs at the two nearest Incans, knocking them off balance. Then they leap through the air and kick the two lifeless leaders square in the chest. **WHAP! WHAP!**

The Incan zombies skid across the ground. Behind them, the remaining warriors fall over like bowling pins, causing a big pile up.

WHUMP! THUMP!

Moments later, the zombies are back on their feet … seemingly unharmed.

"These creatures are unstoppable!" Batgirl shouts.

"We just have to slow them down long enough to stop Rā's," Batman replies.

He reaches into his Utility Belt and pulls out a canister. "This freeze-bomb ought to cool things down," the Dark Knight says. He throws the explosive at the oncoming army.

FWOOOOM!

The bomb covers the Incan warriors in a thick layer of ice—freezing them in place. Suddenly, an ear-piercing scream fills the air.

"*YEEEEAAAAAARGH!*"

The artifact is sucking the life out of Rā's as it brings more warriors back from the dead!

"We need to get that relic before it's too late!" Batgirl cries.

"You need to get to safety," Batman orders his sidekick. "I'll handle the rest."

The two heroes shoot their grapnel guns and swing in opposite directions. Batgirl lands on a nearby ledge where she is out of the newly risen zombies' reach.

Batman zips over a charging warrior and dives through the air at Rā's al Ghūl. The Dark Knight tackles the villain to the ground. *THWUMP!*

Rā's loses his grip on the statue. The ancient relic skitters across the ground and falls into the crevice.

Turn the page.

SHOOOM!

There is another intense blast of light, and the undead warriors slowly melt back into the ground. Ubu hoists himself up just as the floor seals itself shut.

Batman is standing over Rā's when Batgirl joins him. The Demon's Head is now wrinkled, withered, and white. He is barely breathing.

"Master!" shouts Ubu. He picks up the crumpled form of Rā's al Ghūl. "You'll pay for this, infidel!" Ubu curses at Batman.

"We both know that the only way to save Rā's is to bring him back to Gotham City," Batman states. "He will receive excellent care in Arkham Asylum."

"And the two of you can share a cell together if it makes you feel better," Batgirl quips.

Ubu grits his teeth and grudgingly complies. As he follows the heroes to the Batplane, Ubu silently vows that the Society of Shadows will rise again!

THE END

To follow another path, turn to page 17.

The heroes must act fast! Batman whispers something into Batgirl's ear. She nods in agreement.

"Heads up, boys!" Batgirl shouts. The caped crime fighters headbutt their captors. **BONK!**

Free to move, Batman and Batgirl judo flip the ninjas into each other—knocking them out!

The heroes rush toward the Lazarus Pit. Batman somersaults over the mystical pool. He lands in front of Rā's al Ghūl as the madman begins chanting an ancient spell.

The villain's voice echoes through the chamber. Seconds later beams of light shoot out of the relic. The ground and cavern walls begin to shake.

RRRUMMMMBLE!

"There won't be any magic show tonight, Rā's," Batman says. "I'm canceling your performance!"

The villain's glowing eyes focus on Batman. "HA!" Rā's cackles. "You are a mere buzzing insect to me. Did you think you could face off against me while I have the power of a god?"

Turn the page.

"No," Batman replies. "I just wanted to distract you long enough for her!"

Batgirl appears behind Rā's and kicks the artifact out of his hands. ***WHAP!***

"NO!" Rā's screams. The statue of Supay sails through the air. It lands several feet away and slides across the floor into the darkness.

Rā's is enraged. "Very clever, Detective," he spits angrily. "Prepare to test your might against the Serpent's Head!"

Rā's al Ghūl unsheathes his sword. The sharp blade gleams in the light. "You will suffer for this insult!" he yells, lunging at the Dark Knight.

Batman draws out two Batarangs to counter the attack. The weapons clash in a shower of sparks. ***SKEEESH!***

"The Society of Shadows will cleanse the planet and start fresh!" Rā's raves as they battle.

Batgirl rushes to help Batman but slams into a mountain of muscle instead. "Uh, oh," she gulps. "Ubu!"

Turn the page.

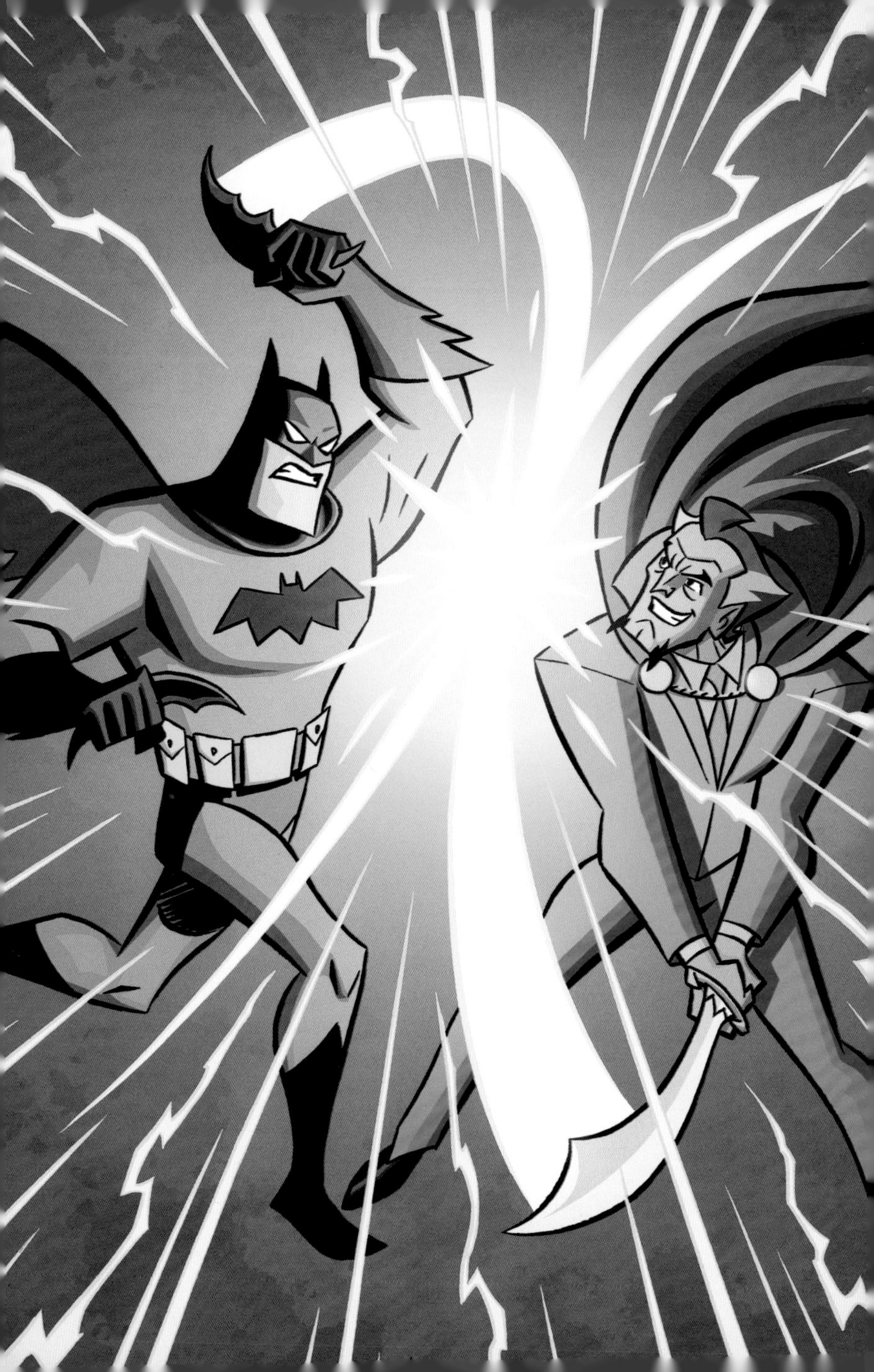

Ubu grunts and takes a swing at Batgirl. But the nimble acrobat backflips out of Ubu's reach, causing him to hit a nearby pillar instead. **BASH!**

"Foolish child," he sneers. "You are no match for me!" Ubu grabs Batgirl's cape and flings her onto the cavern floor. **OOF!**

"So you like to fight dirty?" Batgirl asks as Ubu looms over her. "Well, two can play that game!" She scoops up a handful of dirt and throws it in the bodyguard's face.

"**ACK!**" Ubu chokes and spits out a chunk of dirt. "I will crush you like a bug!"

Batgirl leaps to her feet and pulls out the stun gun from her Utility Belt. "This bug's got her own zapper!" she says. Just as Ubu attacks, Batgirl shocks him with the high-voltage weapon.

ZZZZZZARK! Ubu twitches and slumps over into a smoldering heap.

"The bigger they are, the more fun they are to take down," Batgirl quips. Glancing to her left, she sees a small stone object in the shadows.

Meanwhile, Rā's and Batman continue their battle.

"This defiled world must be restored to its former glory!" the villain yells as he slashes at Batman. But the Dark Knight deflects the blade with his Batarang. *CLANG!*

The villain then kicks Batman into the wall and raises his sword high in the air. "It's a shame you won't be by my side to see my vision become reality," Rā's tells the Dark Knight.

"Here's a reality check for you, Rā's," Batman growls. The hero throws a well-aimed uppercut to send the crazed villain sprawling across the cavern floor.

KA-POW!

The Dark Knight picks up the Serpent's Head and points it at his opponent. "There are less extreme ways to save the environment," Batman says. "My duty is to protect those you seek to harm. Now yield!"

Turn the page.

"NEVER!" spits Rā's. He pulls back his robe to reveal a living cobra coiled around his arm.

In a flash, the cobra leaps at Batman! The Caped Crusader quickly guards his face. The snake digs its poisonous fangs into Batman's armored gauntlet. *HISSSSS!*

The hero wrestles with the reptile as Rā's runs toward the exit. "It appears you're all tied up, Detective," he calls out. "Until next time!" The villain laughs and disappears from the cavern.

Batman grips the snake tightly and flings it onto the ground. Then he sprays it with a strong knockout gas.

FSSSS! The vicious reptile lands limply on the ground.

While the snake snoozes, the Dark Knight races to the temple ruins. He finds his most powerful foe standing at the mountain's edge.

"This is the end of the road, Rā's," Batman shouts. "Give up!"

Rā's al Ghūl smiles wickedly and takes a bow. "This is only the beginning of my journey, Detective," he says. Then he dives off the mountain.

Batman rushes to the edge and watches Rā's plummet into the abyss. The cackling madman is swallowed up by the clouds—then there is silence.

Moments later, Batgirl joins Batman on the mountaintop. "I've secured Ubu and the artifact on the Batplane," she says.

Batgirl sees Batman's grim expression and looks around. "Where's Rā's?" she asks.

"He's fallen off the map," Batman says, pointing over the side. Batgirl gasps.

"He'll be back," Batman assures her. "And the next time the Demon's Head turns up, we'll be ready for him!"

THE END

To follow another path, turn to page 17.

"Let's start at the bottom and work our way up," Batgirl says.

The heroes put on their climbing gear and begin to climb down to the base of the mountain. "Hey, Batman, did you know this mountain is almost eight thousand feet above sea level?" Batgirl adds. "Seven thousand, nine hundred and seventy, to be exact."

"It sure feels like it," Batman grumbles.

Batgirl laughs and says, "Ok, I can take a hint. I'll save the trivia for later."

The terrific twosome continue their descent quietly. Soon an alarm sounds on Batman's tracking device. *BREEP! BREEP!*

"The tracking signal on the stolen relic is extremely strong in this location," Batman says. "We must be very close."

Batman and Batgirl reach the bottom of the mountain. After removing their climbing gear, they trek through the lush green jungle toward the signal.

CRACK! A twig snaps nearby and the heroes stop in their tracks. Something is coming right at them! Batman and Batgirl aim their Batarangs just as the mysterious figure appears.

"A llama!" Batgirl exclaims. "How cute!" The heroes lower their weapons.

"The llama came from a path through these trees," he says. "It appears to be man-made. It looks as if it was hacked out by sharp blades ... like swords used by the Society of Shadows."

"What are we waiting for?" Batgirl asks. "Let's go!"

The duo take the path directly to the clearing in the jungle. There they find Ubu holding the relic and yelling orders.

"Keep digging!" he shouts at a handful of ninjas. "The Demon's Head expects to use the Lazarus Pit soon!"

The henchmen scrape their shovels against the ground.

THUNK! THUNK!

Turn the page.

Batman and Batgirl leap out and surprise the villains. "We're just in time to stop your sinister scheme," Batgirl says. "Where's Rā's al Ghūl?"

"Ha!" Ubu bellows. "Rā's isn't here and you won't find him!"

"We have ways of making you talk," Batman states.

"Is that so?" Ubu laughs. "You'll never take us alive!"

"We'll settle for taking you back asleep," Batman says. He quickly produces a smoke bomb and throws it at Ubu's feet.

PFFFFFFFT! SSSSSSSSSS!

A thick cloud of gas quickly surrounds Ubu and the ninjas. Within seconds they yawn and topple over—fast asleep.

"We may not have gotten the Head of the Demon," Batman says. "But his right hand man makes an excellent consolation prize."

THE END

To follow another path, turn to page 17.

"It looks like Rā's al Ghūl is taking the scroll of Anubis to Egypt," Batman says, pointing at the radar screen. "The country is very dangerous right now," Batman tells his partners. "I'll head over there alone."

Nightwing reluctantly agrees. "Okay," he says. "Batgirl and I will stay here and keep an eye on the other relics."

Batman flies the Batplane toward Cairo, the capital of Egypt. When he arrives, he lands the sleek plane in the desert. Then he heads toward the outskirts of the city, to a historical site known as the Tomb of Anubis.

It is early morning, and Batman has yet to come across any civilians. He swings across the rooftops on his Batrope, following the tracking signal on his portable Batcomputer. It leads him to an abandoned shack.

Suddenly a woman in sunglasses and a headscarf exits the shack and scurries away. The tracking signal moves along with her!

If Batman follows the mystery woman, turn to page 90.
If he investigates the shack, turn to page 102.

Batman races across the rooftops while following the woman. He leaps to the ground and lands in front of her. *FWOOSH! THUD!*

"Still doing your father's dirty work, Talia?"

"No," the woman replies. "I'm doing your dirty work!" She pulls back her scarf to reveal her true identity.

"Catwoman!?" Batman exclaims.

"In the fur," Catwoman purrs back. "I hitched a ride on the Spooky Society's aircraft after they crashed the museum party. I managed to get the scroll that they stole."

She hands the priceless parchment to Batman.

"Why would you do that?" he asks.

"Let's just say that I've always wanted to see Egypt and couldn't pass up the free ride," the thief answers.

"Catwoman, you're in grave danger," Batman tells her. "The Society of Shadows is ruthless and unforgiving!"

Just then, a team of ninjas rushes out from the alleys and drop from the rooftops. They surround Batman and Catwoman.

"HYAAAAAH!"

"I was hoping to avoid them," Catwoman says to Batman. "I guess the cat's out of the bag!"

The feline felon unfurls her whip as the ninjas charge in with swords raised. With cat-like speed, Catwoman snares one man's wrist with her whip and drags him forward. He yelps and falls flat on his face. *WHUMP!*

Batman flings a Batarang and knocks the sword out of a second ninja's hand. The masked fighter trips over the first ninja, sending swords skittering across the ground toward Batman and Catwoman.

They pick up the weapons and cross blades with more oncoming attackers. *CLANG!*

Catwoman knocks out a ninja with the hilt of her sword. *BAM!*

Turn the page.

Meanwhile, Batman expertly takes on three ninjas at once. He thrusts and dodges nimbly between them, striking the weapons out of their hands.

SLASH! CLANG! BANG! Batman delivers three devastating blows that send the ninjas sprawling backward into their comrades.

But the ninjas quickly recover. They gather around the costumed adventurers and overpower them. They drag the duo back to the shack Batman spied earlier. Two guards lead the captives down a narrow staircase into a dark tunnel. After a few feet, Batman leans over to Catwoman.

"Follow my lead," he whispers.

Batman elbows the guard behind him in the face. Then he hurls him over his shoulder with a judo throw. ***WHAP! BAM!*** The ninja lands on his back and lies still.

Catwoman drives her heel into the foot of the guard behind her. Then she follows through with a roundhouse kick to send him crashing into the wall. ***SMASH!***

Moving quickly and silently, the duo disguise themselves with the guards' clothing. Then they dash down the tunnel and slip into a group of ninja fighters unnoticed.

There is a glowing pool full of green liquid in the center of the room. "Is that what I think it is?" Catwoman whispers.

"Yes, it's a functioning Lazarus Pit," Batman says.

At one end Ubu and Talia watch as Rā's al Ghūl rises from the shimmering liquid.

"Now that I feel reborn, it's time to conjure Anubis, the Egyptian god of the dead!" announces Rā's.

The trio walks to an altar holding a golden sarcophagus. Rā's begins chanting an ancient spell.

"Ugh, I've never liked dogs," Catwoman hisses. "I have an idea. This time you follow my lead."

The masked duo sneaks away and climbs onto a rocky crag overlooking the cavern.

Turn the page.

Rā's sprinkles some magic powder over the sarcophagus and continues to chant. Suddenly, a blinding light shines from across the cavern.

A feline figure with a long cloak stands silhouetted against it. "WHO DARES TO DISTURB MY REST!?" the figure roars.

Rā's al Ghūl stops the ritual and confronts the mysterious being. "Who are you?" he asks.

"I AM BAST!" comes the response. "Defender of the pharaoh ... and protector of cats!"

The mystery figure is really Catwoman standing in front of Batman's high-intensity Bat-flashlight.

"Perhaps you woke up the wrong god?" Ubu asks Rā's.

"Nonsense!" spits the Head of the Demon. "I never make a mistake!"

"Foul creature!" Catwoman shouts. "You have defiled this sacred ground with your black magic—and you shall suffer!"

She raises her arms and red flames burst from her hands. **_FWOOSH!_** The ninjas cower in fear.

Catwoman is holding Batman's emergency flares. She hurls them toward the ninjas.

"Fireballs! Let's get out of here!" The superstitious henchmen flee for the exit.

The duo shed their disguises and drop off the ledge. Rā's al Ghūl gazes at his foes with admiration and fury.

"Aha, Detective!" he exclaims. "Your knack for theatrics may have interrupted my plan. But it's only a minor setback. I've come too far to allow you to stop my plans."

"The only place you're going is back to Gotham City," Batman states. "And straight into Arkham Asylum."

"What a pity," Rā's laments. "I had such high hopes for you, Detective. You're the only man I've met that matches my abilities. You could be the next leader of the Society of Shadows."

"I don't think so," Batman replies.

"Then you have sealed your fate," Rā's says. "Eliminate them!"

Turn the page.

"Yes, Master!" Ubu says. "I will exterminate these pests." He and Talia spring into action.

Ubu lunges at Batman, but the Dark Knight sidesteps the attack and karate chops the bodyguard. *CRACK!*

Ubu stumbles but regains his balance. Batman takes another swing at Ubu, but the muscleman grabs Batman's fist in the palm of his hand.

"Infidel!" Ubu snarls, throwing Batman into the wall. *WHAM!* The Dark Knight slumps to the floor.

Talia rushes at Catwoman with a jump kick. "You're no match for me," she says. "I have years of Society training."

However, Catwoman's reflexes are too quick. She drops low to avoid the strike. "And I have a knack for landing on my feet," Catwoman says. "Unlike you."

She sweeps the back of Talia's legs, sending her crashing to the ground. *THUD!*

Catwoman pounces on her prey. Talia struggles to keep the feline fighter's sharp claws at bay.

Turn the page.

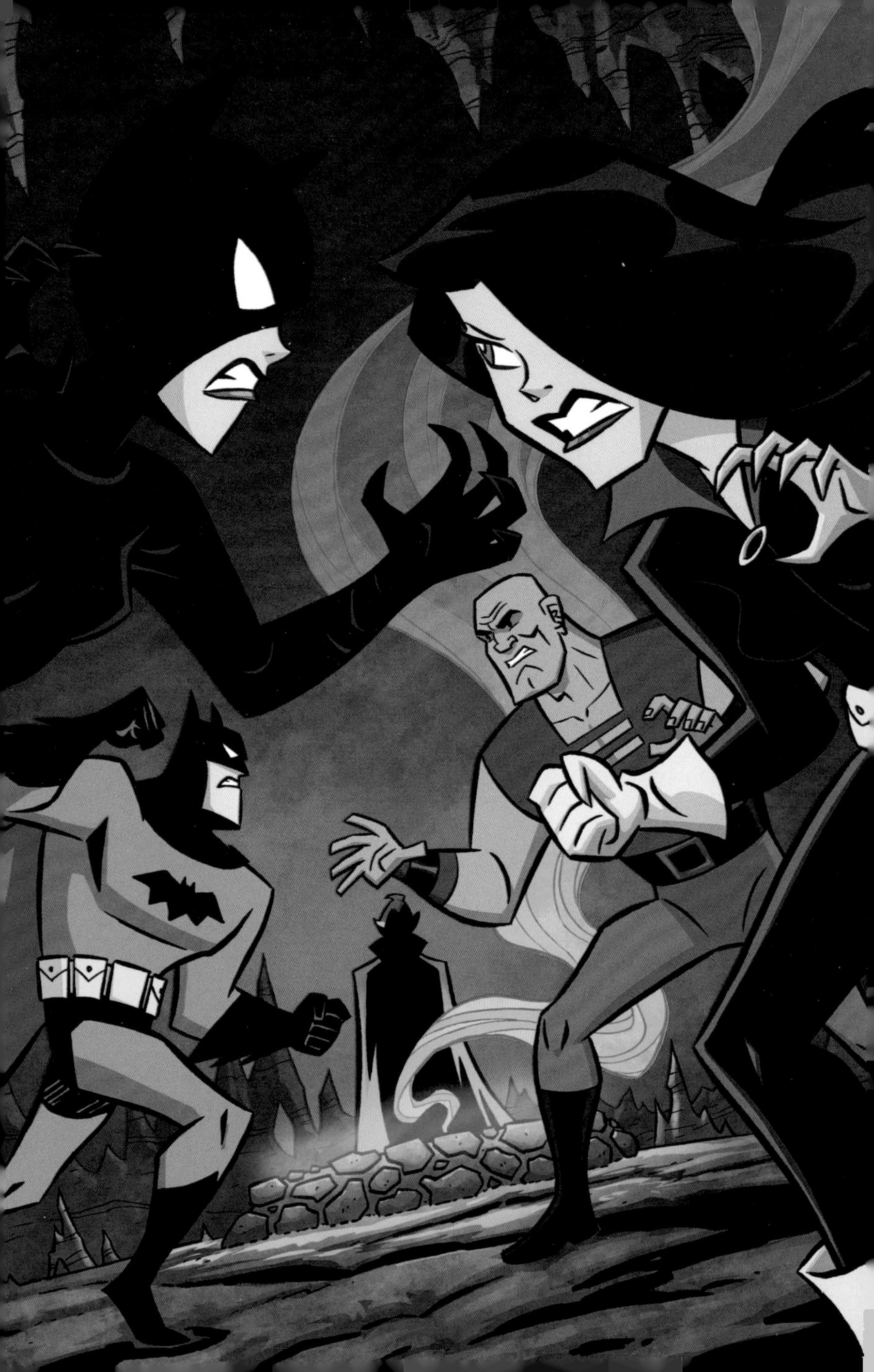

Meanwhile, Batman rolls onto his back and is slightly dazed.

"Still alive?" Ubu taunts. "I will crush you like an insect!"

Suddenly, Batman grabs Ubu's foot and pushes him off. In an instant, the Dark Knight stands up and pummels Ubu with a flurry of punches. But the huge muscleman is hardly fazed.

"That tickles!" Ubu laughs and headbutts the Caped Crusader.

CRUNCH! Batman reels back but ducks just as Ubu swings for a knockout punch. The menacing manservant's fist collides with a stone column.

CRACK! The column crumbles from the force of impact. Stone fragments rain down as the cavern trembles.

SMASH! CRASH! A huge boulder lands between Batman and Ubu, nearly crushing them both.

"We need to get out of here, NOW!" Batman yells.

The enemies stop fighting and run toward the exit. Talia stops to look back.

"Father!" she cries. "What are you doing?"

Rā's al Ghūl stands over the Lazarus Pit. "Do not fret, my daughter," he says calmly. "The Society of Shadows shall rise again … more powerful than ever!"

Rā's dives into the mystical pool. **SPLASH!**

Talia and Ubu move toward the Lazarus Pit as the ceiling begins to cave in.

"Not so fast," Batman says. He and Catwoman grab the two villains and drag them out of the cavern as it collapses. **KRA-KOOM!**

When the dust settles, Batman snaps the Bat-cuffs on Talia and Ubu. He leads the captives back to the Batplane.

"This isn't over," Talia tells Batman. "My father will return again."

"I don't doubt that," Batman replies. "But until then, the two of you can wait for your reunion at Blackgate Penitentiary in Gotham City."

Turn the page.

A week later, Bruce Wayne and his friends are soaking up the sun on a beach in Greece. With no activity from the Society of Shadows, they are able to relax.

"This was the purr-fect idea," Selina says.

"It sure is nice to travel for pleasure and not business for a change," Dick says.

"I've been buried in too much work," Bruce replies with a smile.

"I agree," Barbara adds. "It's nice to get away from it all, even for a short while."

Suddenly, Bruce feels a cold twinge down his spine. He turns to look behind him. High on top of a craggy mountain overlooking the sea, he sees the figure of a man in a fluttering green robe. Then, just as suddenly, the mysterious figure is gone.

It's probably just my imagination, Bruce thinks. But some things don't stay buried for long ...

THE END

To follow another path, turn to page 17.

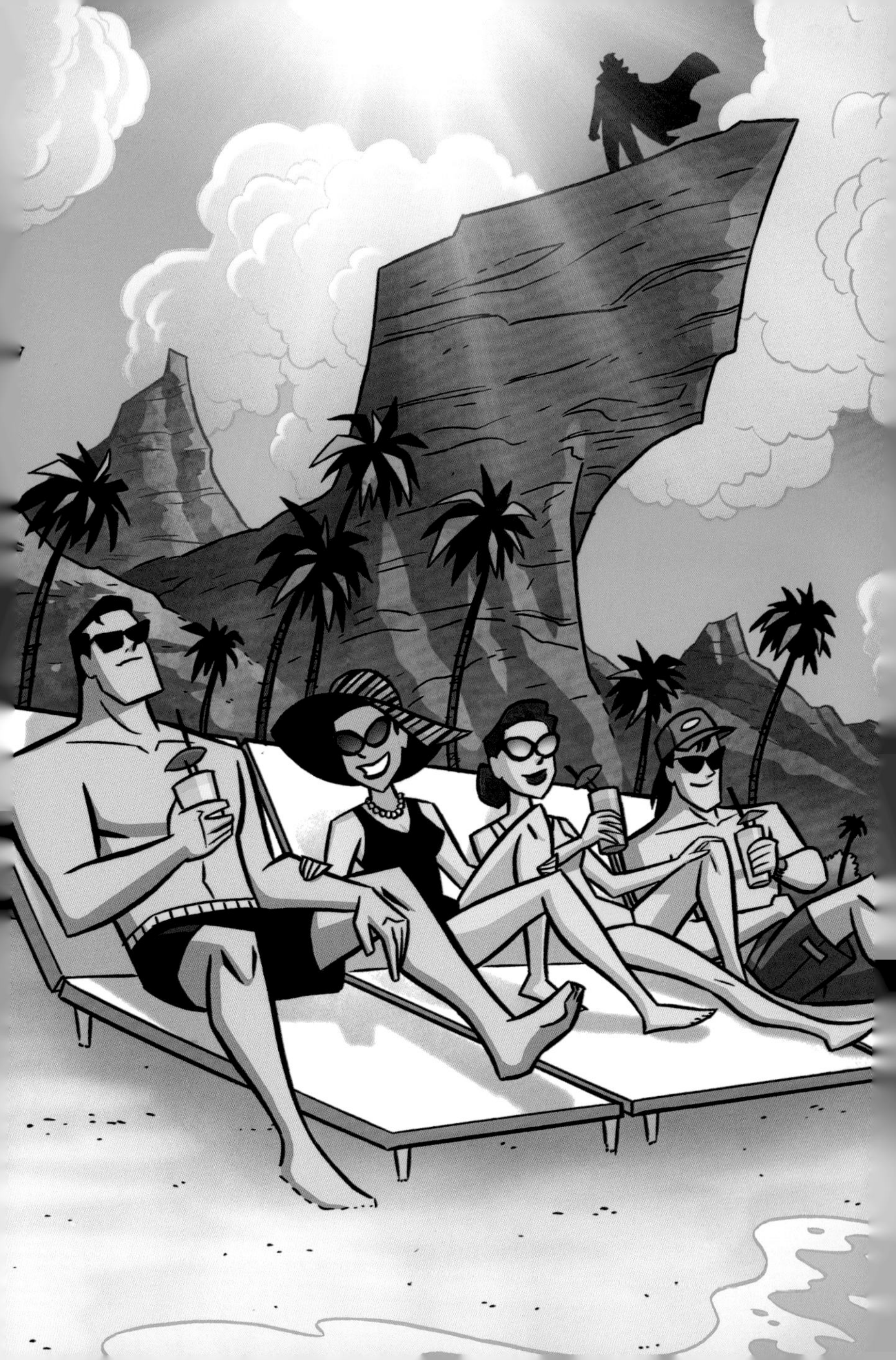

That must be Talia, Batman thinks to himself. *She's led me right to the Society of Shadows!*

Batman leaps off the building and glides down to the ground. **WHOOOSH!**

He lands quietly and enters the shack. To Batman's surprise, the dark room is completely empty! He switches on the night-vision in his cowl's lenses.

Suddenly, two ninja guards appear behind the Dark Knight. They unsheathe their swords and charge. But Batman blocks the blades with the armored gauntlets on his wrists.

CLANG! CLANG! The Dark Knight quickly disarms his attackers.

"You will pay for this, infidel!" yells one of the ninjas. He grips Batman in a headlock. The Caped Crusader breaks free and hurls the ninja over his shoulder with a judo throw—right on top of the other guard. **WHAM!**

With the two men in an unmoving heap, Batman continues his search. He discovers a trap door in the floor and opens it.

Batman follows a narrow winding staircase deep underground. It leads him to a large cavern lit by torches along the rock walls. In the center of the room is a glowing pool of green liquid. It is surrounded by ninjas.

That's a functional Lazarus Pit! Batman realizes.

Standing on the edge of the pit is Ubu. He watches Rā's al Ghūl emerge from the shimmering liquid.

"Now that I feel reborn, it's time to put my plan in motion!" announces Rā's.

Ubu hands Rā's his robe. Then they walk to a gold sarcophagus on an altar at the far end of the cavern.

"Once I call forth Anubis, the God of the Dead, the Society of Shadows will cleanse the planet and start fresh!" Rā's exclaims. His maniacal laughter echoes off the cavern walls.

"The only fresh start you're getting is in a cell at Arkham Asylum!" yells Batman.

Turn the page.

Rā's whirls around in a rage. He sees Batman at the entrance of the cavern.

"Well, well, Detective. You're just in time for the beginning of the end!" the madman says with glee.

"I don't think so, Rā's," Batman states. "I'm here to stop you."

"Your persistence is both admirable and infuriating," sneers Rā's al Ghūl. "Get him!"

On their leader's command, the ninja soldiers charge into battle. "*HYAAAAAH!*" they yell.

The Dark Knight is outnumbered, but he acts quickly. He pulls out a handful of smoke pellets and throws them on the ground.

FSSSSSSSSS! A thick cloud of smoke fills the cavern, blinding the ninjas. But the Caped Crusader's night-vision allows him to see clearly.

WHAM! BAM! WHAP! By the time the smoke clears, Batman is the last man standing. Twenty ninja guards lay unconscious at his feet.

"Thanks for the warm up," he says to Rā's al Ghūl.

Batman shoots his grapnel gun at the cavern's ceiling and swings over the Lazarus Pit to face his archenemy.

WHOOSH! "Now it's your turn, Rā's," Batman growls.

The villain cackles in his adversary's face. "Your arrogance will be your downfall. I told you, this was only the beginning."

As the madman turns to walk away, Batman notices that Ubu is missing. But it's too late. Two heavy fists crash down on Batman's head.

CLUNK! Everything goes dark.

When Batman recovers, he finds himself alone in the cavern. Rā's al Ghūl has escaped. And thanks to the powers of the Lazarus Pit, he's now stronger and more powerful than before.

"This isn't over yet," Batman vows. "I won't rest until I find the Society of Shadows and bring them to justice!"

THE END

To follow another path, turn to page 17.

AUTHOR

New York Times bestselling author John Sazaklis enjoys writing children's books about his favorite characters. He has also illustrated Spider-Man books and created toys used in *MAD* magazine. To him, it's a dream come true! John lives with his beautiful wife and daughter in New York City.

ILLUSTRATOR

Ethen Beavers lives and works in Modesto California. He is best known for his work on the DC Super Friends Little Golden Book series at Random House, as well as the New York Times Bestselling series NERDS at Abrams publishing. He has also illustrated books and comics on titles like Samurai Jack, Batman, Star Wars, and Indiana Jones.

GLOSSARY

archenemy (arch-EN-uh-mee)—one's main or principal foe

asylum (uh-SYE-lum)—a hospital for people who are mentally ill and cannot live by themselves

hieroglyphs (HYE-ruh-glifs)—pictures or symbols used in the ancient Egyptian system of writing

idol (EYE-duhl)—an image or statue worshiped as a god

projectile (pruh-JEK-tuhl)—an object, such as a bullet or missile, that is thrown or shot through the air

pummel (PUHM-uhl)—to punch someone or something repeatedly

relic (REL-ik)—something that has survived from the past

sarcophagus (sar-KAH-fuh-guhs)—a stone coffin

silhouette (sil-oo-ET)—a dark outline seen against a light background

Utility Belt (yoo-TIL-uh-tee BELT)—Batman's belt, which holds all of his weaponry and gadgets

ward (WOHRD)—a person who is under the care of a guardian

RĀ'S AL GHŪL

Real Name:
Unknown

Occupation:
International
Ecoterrorist

Base:
Varies

Height:
6 feet 5 inches

Weight:
215 pounds

Eyes:
Green

Hair:
Gray and White

Rā's al Ghūl has lived for centuries. He has seen the world change over the years, but his beliefs stay the same. He is dedicated to restoring Earth to its original, pristine form. To achieve this goal, Rā's will do whatever it takes, even if that means wiping out all of humanity in the process. Rā's has a legion of followers, including his daughter, who would readily give their lives to see his dream become a reality. His faithful and musclebound bodyguard, Ubu, can always be found nearby.

- Rā's al Ghūl regularly bathes in the Lazarus Pits to maintain his youthfulness and prolong his life. However, he often becomes temporarily insane when he emerges from the Pits.

- Rā's al Ghūl has lived for countless years. He has amassed a wealth of knowledge during his lifetime. His longevity has allowed him to master many fighting disciplines as well, making him extremely dangerous.

- Talia al Ghūl is a firm believer in her father's cause, and she would do anything to help. But she has feelings for the Dark Knight, which often conflict with her responsibilities as Rā's al Ghūl's daughter.

- Rā's sees Batman as his equal, and he hopes to one day convince the Dark Knight to become husband to his daughter, Talia, and heir to his throne. In turn, Batman hopes to one day convince Rā's to help humanity rather than harm it.

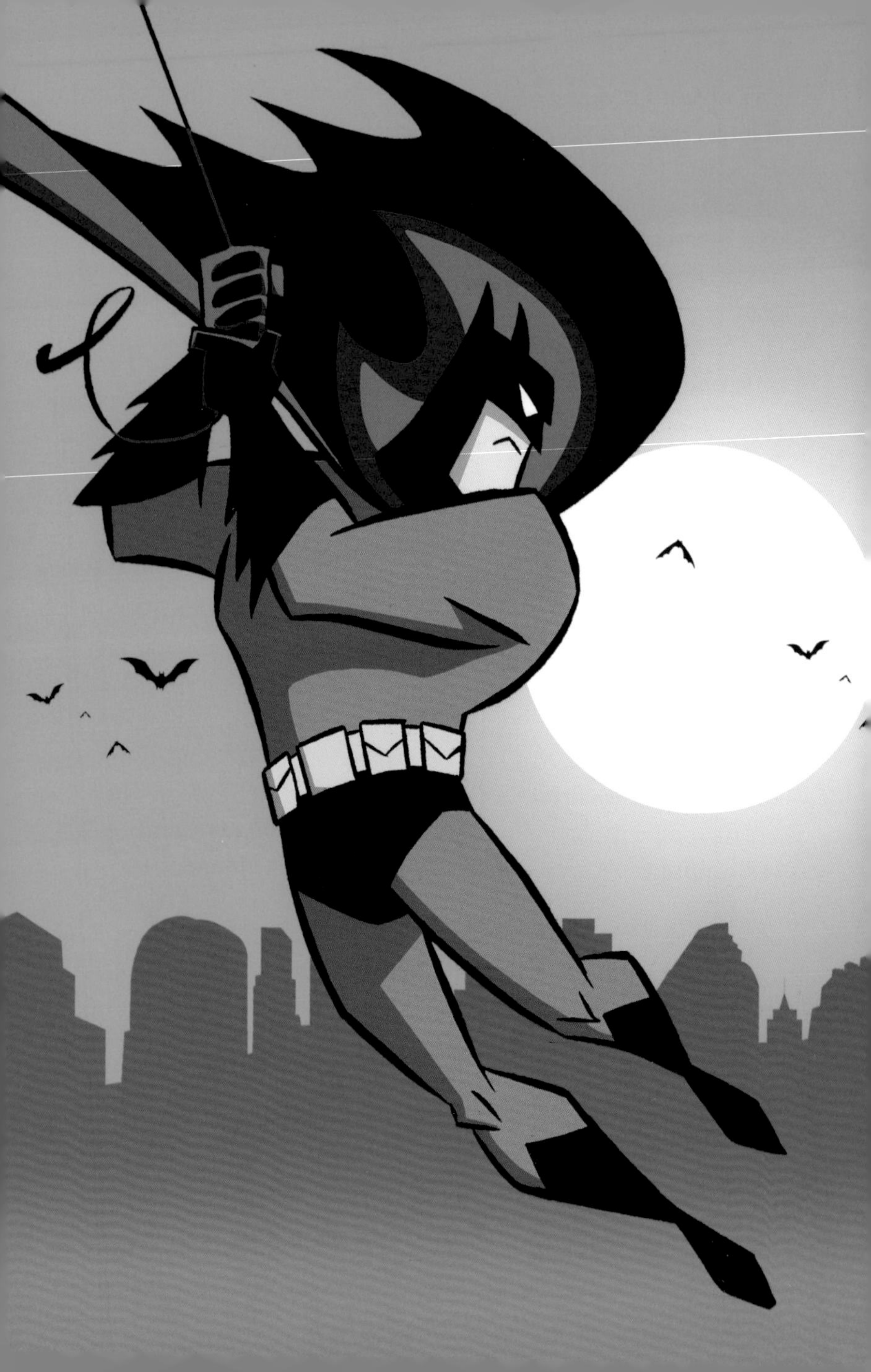